A Tangle in the Vines

Calla Lily Mystery #2

Anna Celeste Burke

A Tangle in the Vines
Copyright © 2019 Anna Celeste Burke
desertcitiesmystery.com

Independently Published

All rights reserved. No part of this work may be reproduced without written permission of the publisher except brief quotations for review purposes.

This is a work of fiction. Names, characters, businesses, places, events and incidents are either the products of the author's imagination or used in a fictitious manner. Any resemblance to actual persons, living or dead, or actual events is purely coincidental. The use of any real company and/or product names is for literary effect only. All other trademarks and copyrights are the property of the respective owners. The author derives no compensation or other benefits from the mention of any company or product.

Cover by Alchemy Book Covers & Design

ISBN: 9781695469594

Books by USA Today and Wall Street Journal Bestselling Author Anna Celeste Burke

A Dead Husband Jessica Huntington Desert Cities Mystery #1
A Dead Sister Jessica Huntington Desert Cities Mystery #2
A Dead Daughter Jessica Huntington Desert Cities Mystery #3
A Dead Mother Jessica Huntington Desert Cities Mystery #4
A Dead Cousin Jessica Huntington Desert Cities Mystery #5
A Dead Nephew Jessica Huntington Desert Cities Mystery #6 [2019]
Love A Foot Above the Ground Prequel to the Jessica Huntington Desert Cities Mystery Series

Cowabunga Christmas! Corsario Cove Cozy Mystery #1
Gnarly New Year! Corsario Cove Cozy Mystery #2
Heinous Habits! Corsario Cove Cozy Mystery #3
Radical Regatta! Corsario Cove Cozy Mystery #4
Bogus Bones! Corsario Cove Cozy Mystery #5 [2020]

Murder at Catmmando Mountain Georgie Shaw Cozy Mystery #1
Love Notes in the Key of Sea Georgie Shaw Cozy Mystery #2
All Hallows' Eve Heist Georgie Shaw Cozy Mystery #3

A Merry Christmas Wedding Mystery Georgie Shaw Cozy Mystery #4

Murder at Sea of Passenger X Georgie Shaw Cozy Mystery #5

Murder of the Maestro Georgie Shaw Cozy Mystery #6

A Tango Before Dying Georgie Shaw Cozy Mystery #7

A Canary in the Canal Georgie Shaw Cozy Mystery #8 [2019]

A Body on Fitzgerald's Bluff Seaview Cottages Cozy Mystery #1

The Murder of Shakespeare's Ghost Seaview Cottages Cozy Mystery #2

Grave Expectations on Dickens' Dune Seaview Cottages Cozy Mystery #3

A Farewell to Arms in Hemingway Hills Seaview Cottages Cozy Mystery #4 [2019]

Lily's Homecoming Under Fire Calla Lily Mystery #1

A Tangle in the Vines Calla Lily Mystery #2

Fall's Killer Vintage Calla Lily Mystery #3 [2020]

The Vintner's Other Daughter Calla Lily Mystery #4 [2020]

Dedication

To all of us who work as hard as Lily does to unravel the tangles in our lives and get to the root of the problem.

Contents

Acknowledgements	ix
Cast of Characters	x
1. A Tangle in the Vines	1
2. Penney Lincoln's Reappearance	12
3. Slimy Chic	21
4. Bag Lady	30
5. The Numbers Man	43
6. Loco Parentis	53
7. Three Ring Circus	64
8. AWOL	69
9. Billie's Bombshells	84
10. Boy Crazy	97
11. Dustin's Debut	108
12. Countdown to Murder	120
13. A Wappo Curse	129
14. Property Matters	137
15. Faint or Feint?	149
16. Another Lincoln	161
17. Dying Declaration	175
18. A Sacred Place	186
19. The Shack	197
20. Untangling the Vines	209
Recipes	223
About the Author	229

Acknowledgements

Thanks to my husband who listens as I read chapters to him and always willing to give me feedback when I hit a snag along the way. He's a constant source of love, support, and inspiration. The best man I ever met.

Thanks as well to the amazing Peggy Hyndman. She works way too hard because so many of my author friends, and I depend on her. Peggy's got a keen eye, a quick mind, and a great ability to tell me in the nicest way that I've got something out of whack!

I'm also so grateful to have discovered Keri Knutson with Alchemy Book Covers & Design. She not only produced the beautiful cover for this book but has gone back and redone all my book covers. She's an artist!!

My ARC Angels are a very special group of readers—some of whom have been with me since I published my first book in 2013. I am a very fortunate author to have their feedback and support.

Cast of Characters

[Note to readers—**skip this section** if you prefer to discover the characters rather than meet them in advance. If you want to check "who's who" among members of this ensemble cast, please do!]

Lead Characters

Lillian Callahan—"Calla Lily," as she was called by her Aunt Lettie, is in her early thirties. An actress with a lead role in *Not Another Day*, a long-running daytime soap opera, her character was killed off in the previous season. When her great Aunt Lettie died, Lily returned to California's wine country where she spent much of her youth. She inherited her aunt's estate including the Calla Lily Vineyards & Winery.

Deputy U.S. Marshal Austin Jennings saved Lily's life when they first met. He's an affable, handsome, lawman who's instantly smitten with Lily. His assignments include apprehending wanted fugitives, protecting federal judges, transporting federal prisoners, protecting federal witnesses, and managing assets seized from criminal enterprises. He also gets entangled, one way or another, in Lily's troubles.

Judy Tucker is a hard-working, elderly rancher who was Aunt Lettie's best friend. She's tough, funny, and handy in the kitchen, the garden, and with tools after years of managing her large ranch.

Letitia Morgan—Aunt Lettie—now deceased, was a strong, independent woman from Alabama who was considered the "black sheep" in family with deep roots in the Old South. She raised Lily when, at age twelve, her parents found her too much to handle. Starting with very little, Lettie built the vineyard and winery and left Lily a substantial estate.

Jesse Hargrove is the Vineyard Foreman/Manager and has a role in maintaining security on the vineyard property where Lily's house is located.

Lily's Diva Posse Members/Calla Lily Players

Zelda Gomez a Latina woman in her late thirties who oversaw hair, makeup, and "ego-wrangling" on the set of *Not Another Day*. She performed in an improv group, has a background in dance, and knows a lot about what goes on backstage.

Melody Skidmore is an actress and had a recurring role on *Not Another Day*. Her character was killed off at the beginning of the current season. She worked as an assistant to a costume designer and for a props master.

Julie Hemsley is a writer on *Not Another Day* and worked as a production assistant before landing the job as a writer. She's also written scripts and plays. Some have been optioned but none were ever produced.

Carrie Cramer is a TV personality with a background in investigative journalism and has dabbled in acting. She currently works a sports journalist in LA and frequently covers the LA Angels baseball team.

The Law

U.S. Marshal, Rikki Havens is Austin's boss. She's asked to assist when local authorities discover the seriousness and complexity of the crimes committed in Calistoga.

Deputy Dahlia Ahern is a member of the Napa County Sheriff's Department.

Officer James Brady is a member of the Calistoga Police Department.

Ben the "Hazmat Man" is a crime scene investigator.

Colin Brinkley is a lawyer and judge. He was a longtime suitor and close friend of Aunt Lettie.

New to the cast in this mystery

Billie Dundee, a twelve-year-old boy caught as an intruder.

The Numbers Man a mysterious man Billie Dundee has met in the woods behind the

Calla Lily Vineyards.

The "Sitter" another mystery man, known to the Numbers Man by that name.

Mick Daley is a set designer recently from *Not Another Day*.

Diane Constantine, a social worker with the county Children's Services.

Rachel and Bud Lincoln are parents of one of the murder victims.

Lydia Wainwright is Billie's teacher who fails to report for duty when school starts.

1

A Tangle in the Vines

"**P**ULL HARDER!" JUDY Tucker shouted.

"I'm pulling as hard as I can," I replied, hollering to be heard above the pounding rain and rolling thunder. A freak storm for this time of year, the rain had been falling for two days almost without pause. Another peel of thunder followed as lightning spread across the night sky, shattering it into pieces.

"Can I help?" Judy asked, moving to my side and speaking almost into my ear. "The water's still rising down below. What's going on?"

"I can't tell. Vines and branches must be tangled around something in the pipe. I'm going to try digging underneath the tangle and beneath the pipe. Maybe that will help. Then I'll go back to yanking at the branch that's sticking out. So far, what I've removed is mostly rotting wood and leaves."

"Rotten is right. It smells like my compost bin. There must be a huge clog in there to have caused the pipe to burst the way it did." Judy turned to look at more of the pipe behind me. The rupture had created two openings in the three-foot pipeline, pushing them apart and leaving them set at odd angles poking up out of the mud.

When Judy said the water was getting deeper, she was talking about a problem behind the backstage building my Aunt Lettie had built as part of an outdoor theater complex. Attached to the stage set front and center in a semicircle of seats arranged in rows, the theater building and basement include dressing rooms, meeting rooms and rehearsal space, storage, equipment, and supplies needed during a live production. It's the fear of damage to the building and its contents that had us out in torrential rain on a dark and stormy night.

We'd been out here for over an hour. The biggest effort underway was piling sandbags around the base of the building to stop water from seeping inside the basement. Lightning arced, closer this time, and made me shudder. I shoveled dirt away from the point where the pipe was clogged. Judy leaned in and eyed the gaping hole. The night sky crinkled with lightning that lit the entire area.

"It's like we're in an old horror film, isn't it, Lily? The storm will be right above us soon. Why don't you leave this and let's go inside? I remember when Lettie had this stormwater system put in. The company she used is still in business. I'll call and get them out here tomorrow. They have a device that can figure out what's causing the problem quickly."

"I want to try a little longer, and then I'll give up. I promise." I gave my Aunt Lettie's best friend a hug. "What if the clog causes the pipe to burst higher up? Who knows what that will do?"

"You're as stubborn as Lettie. I know when I'm licked.

As soon as the last sandbag is down, you're done. I'll have that fine, new man you can't make up your mind about pick you up, and carry you out of here, John Wayne style." Then she laughed hoarsely. She wasn't gone long before that fine, new man she referred to appeared.

"Are you okay, Lily?" Austin asked as he stood at my side in a soaked muddy t-shirt that clung to him. I tried not to let the sight distract me. Judy was right that I was still undecided about what to do about him. The worried expression on his face weakened my resolve to chew him out.

"Judy tattled on me, didn't she? I'd get this done quicker if you two didn't keep checking on me!" As I said that, I leaned in closer to be heard without shouting. His arms were around me in an instant. Austin had made up his mind about me right away, or so he claims.

In a flash of lightning, I could see a smudge of mud on his handsome face that gave him a boyish appearance. I'm a sucker for his vulnerable side and his openness about it. Not that Deputy U.S. Marshal Austin Jennings can't take care of himself.

He'd saved my life, which might also explain how I'd let my guard down enough for him to get this close. My heart beat wildly, betraying my will to get to know him better before succumbing to his charms. "The heart wants what it wants," my writer friend, Julie, insisted when I explained the conflict I felt. My track record with men sucks, and what my head wants is a man I can trust.

"Judy said you seemed tired." As Austin spoke to me, his lips brushed against my cheek. My knees felt wobbly, and I leaned against him.

"I am tired, but I can't be the only one. Please tell me Judy was right that you guys are making progress."

"We sure are, Calla Lily!" My sweet, great aunt gave me that nickname after she took me in when my parents wanted to be rid of me. She gave my nickname to the vineyard and winery that I recently inherited.

"I wish I could say that too." I turned and jabbed angrily at the blockage in the drainpipe with my shovel. More smelly slime slithered out, carrying a small piece of the branch along with it.

"Feisty! There's nothing like a high-spirited filly!" He spoke using a phony cowboy accent that I sometimes find amusing. Under the circumstances, it was irksome.

"I probably stink like a farm animal. Thanks for pointing that out, Cowboy."

"Whoa! You do need a break. Several of Jesse's hired hands are helping with the sandbags now that they finished digging a channel to steer the water back into the drainage system. That's already helping. This whole section of pipe is going to have to be replaced, but once we finish securing the building that'll be the only repairs you'll have to make. I can take over here for a while if you want to rest."

"No, it's getting late. I'd rather keep at it. I'm determined to get this drainpipe unblocked, so it doesn't split again and undo all the work you guys are doing."

I gave Austin a grateful hug and his smile lit up the inky darkness as he held me tighter. Lightning sizzled all around us as if mocking my reaction to his smile.

"I keep pulling small branches, leaves, and even a few rocks from inside the pipe. Then more slides in to replace it. So far nothing appears to be big enough to explain what's preventing water from flowing through the pipe. I guess it's just all tangled around the vines. Judy said the grate should be keeping junk out of the drainpipe. Jesse regularly checks it and would have warned us if there was a problem."

"In this storm, it could have come loose or shifted out of place. Jesse's had his hands full since he came to ask for help, so maybe he hasn't checked it since the pipe burst." That my vineyard foreman had his hands full is an understatement.

When I'd arrived at the end of July, Jesse had been hiring pickers and gearing up for the harvest. The grape harvest continues from August into November, depending on the type of grape a vineyard grows. When grapes are at their peak ripeness, they've got to be picked quickly. The storm hit as Jesse and his hands were hustling to pick the grapes for our Chardonnay and get them to the fermenters at the winery across the street.

Austin didn't say another word but took off sprinting up the slope. I sped after him. The slope had always seemed like a gradual one, but not tonight. In my thirties, I'm not the kid who used to run up and down with friends and climb the fence to get into the woods bordering the property. I was huffing and puffing by the time I caught up with Austin at the top of the slope near the fence between our vineyard and the woods. Rainwater streamed around the opening to the drainpipe instead of flowing into it.

"I'm sorry I didn't ask Jesse to come up here once we located a breach in the pipeline. Judy offered to check, but

I agreed with her that Jesse would have reported a problem if there was one."

"Judy's a great help, but I sent her inside to dry off and see how your divas are doing cleaning up in the basement," Austin said as he pulled a flashlight from a pocket. "If she tells us the water has stopped getting into the basement now that we've installed the first layer of sandbags around the foundation, I want her to stay in there. She can make sure everything stored in the basement is up on the wooden pallets Jesse's field hands hauled down there. I want her to say enough is enough, but you know Judy, she won't do it."

"Judy's as tough as Aunt Lettie was, which is why they were such good friends. Judy has worked hard all her life, and I don't think she understands how to slow down or take breaks. Ranching's a rugged way to live and she's run the entire operation on her own for years." As I said that, Austin aimed the flashlight beam directly into the opening. There was no grate.

"I understand all that," he shouted over the thunder that followed a dazzling lightning display. "Still, the women that matter to me the most aren't always the best judges of their limitations. Do you see what I see?"

A whiff of ozone accompanied another blaze of lightning. I froze. When I didn't answer him, Austin stood up.

"What is it? I didn't mean to insult you or Judy."

"It's not that. I saw something dash into the bushes when the lightning was so bright." Austin shone the beam of his flashlight into the bushes where I pointed. I felt silly. Everything was moving from the wind and rain that whipped through the trees and brush. When there was a pause in the thunder, the wind moaned as if in sorrow or pain. It made my blood run cold. An owl flew from a tree branch above us, and I screeched like a strange bird, startling Austin who turned toward me with the flashlight raised, ready to clobber an intruder. We both laughed with relief.

"Sorry, but you have to admit, I did see something move. I'm not angry, even though I know your comment about Judy was meant for me, too, and not just about how I'm handling this mess tonight."

It had been my crazy idea to stage our first performance of The Calla Lily Players during the November celebration of the harvest. I couldn't take all the credit for the ridiculous decision. My Hollywood pals had encouraged me. The four members of my "diva posse" had driven to the Napa Valley from LA for my great aunt's funeral. When they saw the theater, they'd decided to stick around for a while and urged me to go for the Thanksgiving event!

Even with their help and a few hired hands, trying to put a production together in just over three months was insane. We hadn't counted on Mother Nature kicking us in the pants. It usually doesn't rain heavily around here until December or January, and I can't remember a deluge like this one. If the rain continued, we might be forced to drop the curtain on our play even before it had risen.

"Take a look at this," Austin said. I stared at the grate that was lying in the mud in pieces.

"How could that have happened unless someone deliberately destroyed it? Maybe it's another gift from one of my not-so-tightly-wrapped relatives."

"I doubt it since they've been locked up for months. Whoever you call to make repairs tomorrow, might come up with a clue about how long it's been in this condition. This is recent or Jesse would have noticed," Austin said. "I'll see if he can rig up a cover with chicken wire or something like that for overnight. That might keep anything big from getting into the pipeline again."

"That's a good idea, although I don't see much other than mud and water flowing around the opening, do you?" I bent down and tried to peer over Austin's shoulder as I asked that question. He was squatting and examining pieces of the grate.

Muddy water rushed over his leather cowboy boots. I cringed at the sight. Earlier, when I'd said he should have brought an old pair of work boots to wear in the mud, he'd said, "These *are* a lawman's work boots." Austin took one more look inside the pipe before he stood up.

"The bottom in there is littered with mud and leaves—the stuff you were talking about. I don't see anything very big, but even with my flashlight, it's too dark to see very far into the drainpipe. Believe it or not, some water is flowing slowly. That must mean you've made progress toward dislodging whatever's blocking it."

"Woohoo!" I said sarcastically. "Let me finish the job so we can get indoors and take off these wet, muddy clothes."

"Yes, ma'am! That sounds like a great idea to me!" Austin tore off down the slope. I heard him holler, "Yee-haw."

"That's not what I meant, and you know it!" I shouted, running after him with the muddy water flying as we made loud splashing sounds. When more lightning struck, I picked up my pace. Breathless by the time I returned to the spot where I'd been digging, Austin was waiting. He swept me into his arms and crushed my lips with a soggy kiss.

"I'll go talk to Jesse about creating a makeshift grate for the pipe. As soon as we finish stacking the sandbags, I'll take over here." Austin was about to leave when the sky lit up, and the ear-splitting thunder that followed sent me into his arms with my face buried in his chest.

"That was close!" I cried. He hugged me for a few seconds before stepping around me. Austin bent down and picked something up that was half-buried in the muck. "What's that?" I asked.

"It's an old, broken cassette tape."

"Oh, good grief! Some jerk has been dumping garbage in the woods. It's no wonder the pipe couldn't handle it. I wouldn't be surprised if the boombox that goes with the tape is stuck in there."

"You could be right. Hang in there just a little longer, and then you can call it a night." He gave me a peck on the cheek and left. For a few seconds, I could hear splashing and sucking sounds as his boots trudged through the muddy canals that riddled the area around me. I heard him shouting at someone. It might have been Judy, although I couldn't make out one word of their conversation.

"You, rat!" I hollered at an imaginary foe. "Did you destroy the grate and wreck our drainage pipe to save a few bucks on hauling your garbage away?" I attacked the clog angrily. When I landed a savage blow on the stubborn branch, a chunk broke off. It slid out, bringing trash with it—not a boombox, but books.

For a few moments, lightning and thunder burst around me in almost continuous fury like the grand finale at a fireworks display. In the light, I recognized one of the books—a text I'd used in middle school twenty years ago. How could the garbage be that old without having destroyed the pipe long ago? Staring into the opening of the pipe, I cringed. A tingle like static electricity caused the hair on the back of my neck to stand up.

The straps of an old backpack were hanging halfway out of the pipe, caught on the rest of the oak branch I'd been battering. A chill ran through me as I gave the branch a yank. Nothing happened. When I gave it another tug, the branch came out and so did the backpack. More sludge followed, rife with the odor I'd smelled while driving on LA freeways with the top down on my convertible. I didn't want to do it, but I pulled out my flashlight to examine the opening more closely. If there was a dead animal in there, I didn't want to be surprised. I stopped suddenly. Marlowe was barking.

"Marlowe, what are you doing out here?" I searched the darkness with my flashlight. Even with the help of more lightning, I couldn't see him. "Judy, do you have Marlowe with you?" She didn't answer, or if she did, I couldn't hear her.

Then, I jumped out my skin as something behind me moved. I turned around and caught the gaping, black mouth of the pipeline in the light. For a moment, I imagined something inside gazing at me. The ground beneath the pipe washed away, and it dropped oozing slime and garbage. I let out the breath I'd been holding as the rank odor grew stronger. A faded red baseball cap lay on the ground amid a slurry of wet, faded papers.

"Homework," I muttered. A letter grade was at the top of one of the pages halfway out of the backpack. I bent over, and gasped as I recognized a barely readable name scrawled in the right-hand corner. I jumped, imagining that a ghostly hand had touched me on the shoulder as I read the name again. I felt dizzy, disoriented. "What does this mean?"

In my muddled state of mind, it took a minute for it to register that Marlowe was barking again, furiously now, closer to me. I spun around searching for him, but I couldn't see him. When I heard movement behind me again, I whipped around in that direction. I would have sworn I'd glimpsed a shadowy figure—my ghost was on the run.

"Lillian Callahan, you're losing it!" Then I felt a moment of relief as Marlowe barked so close that I bent down and reached for him. I missed and my feet slid out from under me. As I fell flat on my back, a disturbing, almost human sound came from the drainpipe. It groaned in metallic agony and dumped its contents in a rush. I pushed against the ground with my feet and hands without getting any leverage in the smelly slime. The sludge from the pipe crept toward me.

Marlowe was still barking and growling as he raced up the slope toward the woods. Then I heard him yelp. I frantically tried to get to my feet to go after him, but I froze instead. When I fell, my flashlight had flown from my hand and landed beyond my reach, but it had stayed on. It illuminated a ghastly sight as a hollowed-eyed skull moved closer. What followed was even more horrific.

2

Penney Lincoln's Reappearance

I NEVER SCREAMED louder in my life. Not even on-screen in one of the many scenes where my devious character, Andra Weis, on *Not Another Day* had gotten herself into a fix. I kept screaming and didn't let up as I rolled over and crawled on my hands and knees through the revolting muck until I reached less slimy ground and finally stood up. Flashlight beams bounced around me, already too close to have come simply in response to my screams.

"Don't come near me! I'm covered in filth!" I wailed, imagining that I looked like Carrie in that scene at the prom. "Marlowe's chasing someone! Please get him. I'm afraid he's been hurt." I was sobbing now from terror and sorrow. What would I do if I lost my ten-pound Min Pin with the heart of a hundred-pound wolf? Jesse, Judy, and others I couldn't see flew past me up the path toward the woods.

"They'll get Marlowe," Austin said, staying put. "Judy told us he'd spotted an intruder." I could tell every muscle in Austin's body was primed for the chase, but he didn't leave my side. Even in my anguished state, I felt comforted by his presence. "When you screamed, we were afraid he'd done something to you. I'm glad you're okay, Lily."

"Stop! Put him down!" That was my fiery Puerto Rican friend, Zelda, shouting at the top of her lungs. She issued the command to stop in English and then again in Spanish. A barrage of foul-mouthed curses delivered in Spanish, French, and Italian followed the order. Then a man's voice bellowed in rage and pain. I rejoiced when Marlowe barked. He was alive!

"Grab him, Jesse!" Judy hollered from somewhere in the darkness. "Don't let him get away. Who is he? What's he doing here?"

"Let's hope Jesse tackles him. The answer to Judy's questions must have something to do with that," I said, pointing to an intact body lying on top of old bones not far from a skull. Then, I did something my soap opera character never would have done. I took a step, doubled over and dry-heaved near where I'd crawled out of the muck. I backed up quickly, though, and choked back a scream at another grisly sight.

"Eek, eek! Get off me!" Something was crawling up my arm. I stripped off my rubber raincoat and tossed it onto the ground. The odor it gave off was horrid. I must be losing my mind because Austin pointed his flashlight at me, and there was nothing on my arm.

"What is it?" he asked as I pointed at the ground. He searched the area around my discarded raincoat.

"That! There!" I hollered as a long black centipede slithered from my coat sleeve. I shivered and almost kicked Marlowe as I scooted away.

"Marlowe, thank goodness!" I cried. Normally, he

would have jumped into my arms. He took a sniff, whimpered, and backed off.

"I'm calling Rikki," Austin declared. "I want her to come out here. If the guy who just flew up the hillside is responsible for two dead bodies, maybe authorities already know who he is."

"Three," I corrected him. "There's another one." Austin located the skull near where I'd tried to lose my dinner. This one was only partially visible as it protruded from the muck. "If they know who his, what's he doing out here?"

"That's another reason to get Rikki involved. If he's a fugitive from justice, the U.S. Marshals Service should be in on the investigation from the beginning."

"We lost him," Jesse hollered as he came bounding back down the slope, breathing hard, with the others a few steps behind him. "I called 911 and reported a male intruder on the property who tried to steal your dog before escaping into the woods. The fence must have given way during the storm." The fence had been rebuilt a few months ago when Austin recommended that we upgrade our security. My guess is the same man who just ran away destroyed the grate on the drainpipe and knocked down the fence.

"Marlowe bit him!" Zelda chortled as she and Judy caught up to Jesse.

"He's never done that before!" I exclaimed. "Is he okay?"

"I hope not," Judy replied, shouting to be heard.

"It serves him right! Zelda told him to put Marlowe down. What choice did Marlowe have but to take matters into his own jaws?" Melody asked as she took a step back.

Like the rest of us, my neat-freak diva friend was covered in mud and muck up to her knees. "What is that stench?"

"I'm talking about Marlowe. Is he okay?" I hollered, ignoring Melody's question. I was grateful to get a word in. When everyone shut up, they took Melody's lead, and backed away. Melody leaned over and picked up Marlowe.

"Marlowe's fine, thanks to Jesse. Jesse almost had his hands on the creep, but when Marlowe bit him, he tossed Marlowe like a football. Somehow Jesse changed direction and caught him in the dark."

"Like a first-rate pass receiver in the NFL," Carrie added. An actress, turned, publicist, turned sports journalist, I'm sure she knew what she was saying.

"Thank you, Jesse," I said. "Why grab Marlowe?"

"To keep him—and us—from tracking him as he ran for it," Austin replied. "Hang onto Marlowe, Melody, so he doesn't wander into the crime scene."

"Crime scene? Is that what's causing the disgusting odor?" Melody asked, covering her nose with her free hand.

"Yes, but it's probably me too since I rolled around in the slime pit," I added.

"Not compost, I take it," Judy commented during a pause in the thunder.

"No, I'm afraid not. The good news is the clogged pipe is finally open," I replied, not having to shout too loudly as the storm slackened. "The bad news is…"

"That freak who ran away killed something…" Zelda's voice trailed off as her flashlight settled on the body and she crossed herself. "Or someone."

"More than one someone," I responded. I was about to explain when a huge bolt of lightning hit a tree in the preserve area on the other side of a fence not more than ten yards away. The tree exploded, and screams rang out.

I screamed too, but not because of the fire and noise. There was hatred in the eyes of a man hidden in the brush. I grabbed Austin's arm. Marlowe growled from deep inside his belly. When I looked again, he was gone.

"I saw him," Austin said before speaking to everyone.

"Jesse, I'm glad you called 911. We need the authorities out here right away. Do you want to see if the dispatcher will put you through to Dahlia? I'm going to give my boss, Rikki Havens, a call and see what the U.S. Marshals Service can do to help."

"I'm sure Dahlia will be glad to have all the help she can get. I'm almost certain one of the bodies belongs to a girl who went to middle school with me. She vanished and I never heard what happened to her."

"Are you talking about Penney Lincoln?" Jesse asked, aghast.

"Yes. Her name is on an old worksheet lying in the mud and there are more papers in a backpack that are probably hers. That's got to be the baseball cap she used to wear everywhere she went, don't you think?" Jesse's eyes followed my finger to the hat lying inches from a skull. He didn't speak but nodded in agreement, as he swayed ever so slightly. I was afraid the tall, sturdy man might keel over.

"Are you okay?" Carrie asked him.

"I will be. I just need to walk this off," he added as he stepped away. "We were convinced she'd run away."

"That's what I heard too—that she'd run off with some guy," I said.

"As I recall, the police claimed Penney's disappearance wasn't related to boyfriend trouble because her mother insisted that she didn't have one," Judy said. Jesse and I glanced at each other.

"Did they check with her friends? I wasn't a close friend, but if I'd been asked, I would have told them to check to see if any of her male friends were also missing." Jesse had stopped pacing around. "What about you, Jesse?"

"Maybe her mother didn't know what was going on, but we did. All the buzz at the time was that Penney Lincoln was a girl with lots of boyfriends who ran off with one of them."

"No matter what Penney's mother told the police, she knew better," I said. "I overhead Aunt Lettie tell someone that using almost those exact words."

"Who?" Jesse asked.

"I'm not sure—she was on the phone at the time."

"Clearly, it wasn't me. Of course, I wasn't Lettie's only friend," Judy added.

"Well, whoever Lettie was speaking to had to be a man because she said 'goodnight, handsome' when she hung up the phone in her study," I said.

"I'll tell Rikki that the disappearance of Penney Lincoln is the place to start. Maybe we'll get lucky and a name will pop up to help us figure out who Jesse almost got his hands on tonight." As Austin struggled to place his call in the darkness and rain, the rest of us drifted a little farther away from the awful scene. They kept their distance from me.

"If he's the one who killed Penney Lincoln, how old must he be?" Judy hollered.

"Not that old if he was able to get away from Jesse the way he did. He's in reasonably good shape to have outrun our resident wide receiver." Jesse had recovered enough to get on his phone and place another call to the police. He even managed to smile at Carrie's remark.

"Actually, he doesn't have to be any older than me if he was Penney's age when he killed her or even a little older," I argued. "Maybe they had a lover's quarrel, and it got out of hand and he accidentally…"

"Yeah, right!" Zelda said, cutting me off. "He's the unluckiest man I've ever known if you're saying he killed two other people by accident too." She paused before going on. "You saw the way that dirtbag was looking at you when the firelight caught him hiding behind the fence, didn't you?"

"Yes," I replied.

"If you ask me, I'd say he was trying to decide if you'd fit in the drainpipe."

"Stop it, Zelda! Lily said she saw him. She must already be creeped out. I am." As Melody spoke, she searched the area around us. We all did the same, peering into every dark space. The downpour had eased up, but the bushes and trees still rustled in the breeze. He could have been concealed anywhere.

Austin must have been listening to the exchange between Zelda and Melody. Or maybe I was still close enough to the illumination from my flashlight on the ground to see me shaking. I was chilled to the bone by more than the weather. Zelda hadn't fallen for my lame attempt to deny the truth about the man glaring at me. I'd played the role of a psychopath long enough to recognize one and Zelda knew it. Austin was adamant when he spoke up again.

"Lily, go home, please! Take your diva posse, Judy, and Marlowe with you. Jesse and I will deal with the police. Lock the doors, get cleaned up, and don't open the door for anyone until I tell you to do it, okay?"

"Austin's right. Let's get out of here." Judy urged. I hesitated, hoping to hear what Rikki had to say before I left. I hadn't known her long, but from what I could tell, Austin's boss was a clever, experienced member of the U.S. Marshals service.

"Her track record is strong, and she's got great instincts," Austin had told me before we were introduced a few months ago. There's no question in my mind that Rikki is more competent than Dahlia, an officer with the county sheriff's department. Even if Rikki didn't take a direct role in investigating the case, she'd make it easier for Austin to help.

I'm not sure why I'd slowed things down with Austin. I find him insanely attractive, and there's no one on earth I trust more, professionally-speaking—even with my life. My heart raced as a whiff of smoke reached me, triggering a flashback. The eyes of the man lurking in the brush had bored into me like torches.

Why is he angry with me? I wondered.

"Hey, Rikki, it's Austin. I know it's late, but I've got a situation on my hands." He was silent for a moment. "Um, well, yes. It involves Lily because the bodies are on her property. Three of them. Lily says one of the bodies may belong to Penney Lincoln, a classmate who went missing twenty years ago."

"Rikki's in the loop about Penney Lincoln's reappearance, let's go, okay?" Judy argued. I took a step and then stalled again by leaning over as if clearing something from my shoe. Despite urging me to go, Judy wasn't moving any faster than I was, and she was doing her best to eavesdrop.

"What if Rikki has a question for me? We can't get any wetter than we already are, and this drizzle can wash off some of the crud I wallowed in." Another enormous bolt of lightning and a deafening clap of thunder propelled Judy into drill sergeant mode.

"Let's move! I'd like to stick around and hear more, too. You know what they say about curiosity killing the cat. I'm older than the rest of you so I've used up most of my nine lives already. Our handsome lawman will give us the scoop. If your smile doesn't do it, Lily darling, my cookies will."

We nearly ran the quarter of a mile back to the sprawling two-story ranch house that Aunt Lettie had remodeled into a bed and breakfast. Now that my friends had moved in, there weren't any vacancies. The night air filled my lungs and cleared my head.

Should I send my friends home to LA until this latest disaster in my life has been cleaned up?

If he'd killed Penney Lincoln and had eluded capture long enough to kill again, what kind of a sinister mastermind must he be? I'd been so focused on myself, that it hadn't occurred to me until now that he'd also seen Judy and my diva pals. I love them like family. No way was he going to give us a reason to hang out a vacancy sign.

3

Slimy Chic

I SQUINTED AS my eyes adjusted to the bright overhead lights in the kitchen. We looked like a bunch of drowned rats. Marlowe was a muddy mess too. Melody took him straight to the sink, and when the water was warm, hosed him down. He snapped at the water squirting from the sprayer and did a tap dance, splashing in the water around his feet.

"What happened to you?" Julie asked as she suddenly appeared in the doorway that led from the hallway into the kitchen. She scanned us and then zeroed in on me. Our playwright, Julie, had stayed here in the house trying to complete another draft of the play we planned to debut in November.

Telling her to stay put and focus on rewriting the play was an effort to stay on track for opening night. Julie held Melody's teacup Yorkie, Darjeeling. The pooch was whining and squirming to get to her "mom" or to her best buddy, Marlowe.

"She got up close and personal with a dead body," Zelda snapped.

"More than one," Judy added. Then she wagged a finger at me. "You're stinking up the place."

"I'd stink worse if I hadn't ditched the raincoat after I felt a creepy-crawly thing slithering up my arm." I shuddered. Melody towel-dried Marlowe and handed him to Julie.

"You're not kidding, are you? I need to write some of this into the play—Andra Weis gets her comeuppance!" A staff writer for the soap in which Melody and I both had long-running parts, Julie killed us off—me first and then Melody early this season. Not that it was Julie's fault. She'd argued against it, but staff writers in Hollywood don't win many arguments. My writer diva pal was still ticked off about it, which is one reason she'd decided to "call in well" and take a leave.

"Comeuppance?" I asked not exactly sure what she meant.

"You bet! Andra never minded blood and guts but bugs and stinky mud, uh, no!"

"It's not the bugs you can see that worry me. You need to keep Darjeeling and Marlowe out of here. Who knows what Lily has brought inside with her?"

As Melody's brow furrowed, I suddenly felt itchy all over. The first time her career had stalled years ago, Melody had considered becoming a nurse. She quickly discovered she couldn't stand the sight of blood. Unfortunately, the courses she'd taken had turned her into a germaphobe.

"Melody's right. You need to get out of those clothes and shoes," Judy insisted. "I'd tell you to throw them away, but the police may want them."

"Despite my recent stint as a sports reporter, I've been at enough crime scenes to recognize the odor. The crime scene investigators wear hazmat suits. You don't just need to get rid of your clothes, but you've got to scrub down, or you're going to stink like that tomorrow too. Put your clothes and shoes in a plastic bag and seal it tight for the cops—even your underwear."

"Eew, you're right. It's on my skin," I said after sniffing my arm. Then I pulled a loose strand of hair under my nose. "In my hair too! What am I going to do?"

"If there's hydrogen peroxide in the house, I can whip up something for you to try," Judy offered. "It's a home remedy that works great on skunk odor."

"I use hydrogen peroxide." Zelda kicked off her shoes. "I'll get it. My feet are clean, and dry enough not leave a trail like a slug."

"Then what? I'm too big to fit in the sink like Marlowe. Somehow, I've got to get to a shower."

Judy removed a box of plastic bags from the pantry. The huge ones like we use for yard work. She pulled one from the box and held it up to me. Then she pulled a second one out and searched the pantry until she found a box of gallon-sized freezer bags. After opening the bottom seam on one of the enormous orange lawn bags, she poked holes in it on each side, and handed it to me.

"Put it on—over your head. The other holes are for your arms. Take off everything else you're wearing and drop it into this bag." I was too tired to come up with an alternative, so I did as she asked.

"You could stuff this and turn me into a pumpkin," I said when the big orange bag billowed up as I wrestled to take off my disgusting wet clothes. Marlowe and Darjeeling were quiet as mice and took turns cocking their heads as if trying to understand what the crazy human was doing now. I was getting sweaty from the exertion. Once I'd finished by tossing my shoes and socks into the bag, I used the armholes Judy had made.

"Close the bag tight until we can give it to the police!" Judy ordered as she handed me a rubber band. As soon as I'd secured the bag, Judy offered me a plastic grocery bag. "Stuff your hair up under this and tie the handles together in the front."

"Now, for your feet," Judy added as soon as I'd done my best to turn the grocery bag into a plastic shower cap. She handed me the smaller plastic bags and rubber bands.

"Thanks." I put a foot into each gallon bag and then used the rubber bands to bind them to my ankles.

"Here it is, Judy," Zelda said as she bounded back into the kitchen with a bottle of hydrogen peroxide. She stopped abruptly with her arm still outstretched. I was standing there, awkwardly, with one hand on my hip, waiting to hear what Judy would tell me to do next. "Chica, you're workin' it! That's gonna be a whole new style thing, I just know it."

"What should we call it? Slimy Chic?" I asked. Everyone had a good laugh as I did a fashion model turn. Darjeeling and Marlowe, who must have figured everything was okay, woofed and wagged their tails. Then Carrie spoke up.

"If the show's over, I'm heading upstairs. Dibs on the shower in our apartment over the garage." Barefooted, she'd taken one step when a huge bolt of lightning hit somewhere close. The lights flickered and then went out. In the dark, I could see red and blue police lights flashing through the blinds over the sink.

"Cue the sax, we've just gone from Vaudeville slapstick to film noir," Melody announced.

"Crime jazz, baby," Julie added. "Although the soundtracks to the Chandler and Hammett films didn't come from the streets of LA, but from Hollywood orchestras." Julie also teaches writing classes and loves to share what she's teaching with us—whether we wanted to hear it or not.

"Shush, Julie. I hear someone running through the rain, don't you?" Zelda was right. More than one person was running toward us. The flash of lightning that had killed the lights had come from a different direction. Perhaps the storm had passed us, which explained why the footsteps were audible.

I briefly flashed on the man caught in the glow cast off by flames from the burning tree. In my imagination, the glint of fire in his eyes was more than reflected light. Was he still out there? Was someone running after him? We all shrieked when the dogs barked at what sounded like stormtroopers mounting the steps to the deck. Fists pounded on the door.

"Is everything all right in there?" That was Dahlia's voice. The local constabulary had arrived.

"Lily, it's me. Let us in," Austin added.

"You'd better do it. The Marshal will just kick the door in if you don't." I was about to do as Judy suggested when I remembered the way I was dressed. The frigging orange bag almost reached my knees, so nothing was exposed, but Slimy Chic hadn't become a "thing" yet. "Oh, good grief! He's going to see you looking lots worse than you do now after you two have been married for a while."

"That's not happening anytime soon," I groused and stepped away from the doorway as Judy unlocked it.

"Then it doesn't matter what you look like, does it?" She removed the chain and swung the door open. A pair of high beam flashlights swept the darkness before coming to rest on me.

"Trick or treat!" The snarky local police detective remarked as the lights came back on. She stepped inside, and Austin shut the door as he and a crime scene investigator in full hazmat regalia crowded into the kitchen.

I was tempted to smack the smirk off Dahlia's face. My alter ego, Andra, wouldn't have hesitated. All I needed was to get hauled into jail in this getup. Austin's mouth was hanging open as he stared at me. When I glared at him, he shut his mouth.

"Wow! We need pictures of you in Slimy Chic with the crime scene guy at your side. Julie, hon, you just gotta work this scene into the play!" Zelda whipped out a phone she had in a pocket. Before I could say a word, the guy in the hazmat suit had stepped next to me, and Zelda clicked away.

"Uh, no offense, but you've got the smell of decomp on you. You really need to be decontaminated." He raised the mask that hung around his neck, covered his nose, and inched away. More clicks and giggles as both hands flew to my waist, hiking the up the bag.

"Perfect!" Zelda said. "A little more leg is exactly what

the shot needed."

"You'd better stop, Zelda. She's about to blow her top!" Carrie said, scooting closer to the doorway. I tapped my foot and the plastic rustled.

"So, what pray tell brings you here?" I asked our guests.

"You mean besides the little matter of a dumpsite left by what's most likely a serial killer?" the snippy detective asked.

"If that's the reason for your visit, why aren't you and your helper out there collecting evidence before the storm of the century washes it away?"

"We've tented the area and borrowed some sandbags to contain the runoff as well as we can." Her tone had turned defensive.

"At a second site, in the preserve area too," Austin added almost before Dahlia had finished. The photo-happy crime scene investigator held up a gloved finger.

"To be more precise, the site in the woods is the original dumpsite—at least for the older bodies. Unofficially, I'd say that all but the newest body were moved from the first site to the second site here on this property. By that, I mean the old skulls and bones were stuffed into the drainpipe before the most recent body was deposited in there as well."

"Why?" I asked.

"This is merely speculation at this point, but I'd say coyotes!" He paused as if for effect or waiting for us to get it. I had a hunch, but Judy posed a question pulling it all together.

"They dug up the bones, the rain carried them down

the slope, and the killer found himself with a problem on his hands, right?"

"Excellent! Some version of your scenario would be my guess, yes. I do mean guess, so please don't quote me on anything I've just said. If you do, I'll say you're nuts." He arched one eyebrow as he fixed his gaze on me. I ignored him, itching quite literally, to decontaminate myself. To do that, I had to come up with some way to get Dahlia to postpone taking our statements until tomorrow.

"The newest victim can't have been dead long. It's obvious she's a woman, do you have any idea who she is?" I asked.

"From a name tag or the driver's license in her hand?" Dahlia snapped. I was immediately sorry I'd asked. Apparently, Marlowe objected to Dahlia's tone and growled at her.

"You'd better not tick him off. He's already taken on one unwelcome intruder tonight." Melody took Darjeeling from Julie and then rubbed Marlowe's little head as she said that.

"Ooh, snap!" Zelda said. That set Dahlia off.

"We know that! Austin told us some guy grabbed Marlowe. It's because Marlowe bit him that we're here. That and the fact that Austin took off when he saw the house go dark."

It was Dahlia's turn to tap the floor with her foot. My inner Andra was crying out to wring Dahlia's neck when I suddenly felt sorry for Austin. Standing there in a poncho issued to him by the crime scene investigators, he still had mud on his face. He had to be exhausted and yearning for a shower as much as I was.

That'll teach you to come over for a Friday night dinner and a movie with the jinx I've become! I thought as we made eye contact. It had to be more than plain old bad luck that he was here when all hell broke loose in my life—again.

"What do you want with Marlowe?" Julie asked, taking a step back and hugging him closer.

"I'd like to check him over in case there are fibers on him from the contact with the mystery man who may or may not be the killer."

"Too late, Hazmat Man!" Melody replied, testily. "I already gave him a bath."

"That is unfortunate. Has he had anything to eat or drink?"

"Water from the sprayer I used when I hosed him down in the sink," Melody replied.

"We haven't had a chance to feed him," I stammered feeling like a neglectful mother.

"Marlow had water and food backstage before I brought him outside to do his business. That's right before he took off after that guy who was standing behind you, Lily."

"Standing behind me? When?" Could he have been that close without me even knowing it?

4

Bag Lady

"When Marlowe started barking, I couldn't understand why he was upset," Judy explained. "He got away from me and when lighting hit, I caught a glimpse of a man in a hoodie standing right behind you. By then, Marlowe had already taken off running. When you screamed, I thought the guy had grabbed you or hurt you. That's what I told Austin until we saw you were okay."

"I'm going to be sick!" I said. A flood of recollections crowded in on me—the noises behind me, an imagined touch on the shoulder, and a figure in shadow that vanished. Dahlia reached for the orange trash bag near her.

"No, no! Not that one!" Several people said at the same time.

"That bag is for you, Hazmat Man." Julie smiled at him in a playful way. He didn't appear to know how to respond.

"We'll all be sick if you open that in here," Carrie added.

"It's Ben, please. Why is it you seem so familiar to me? I'm not great with names, but I never forget a face."

I rushed to the sink, not waiting for Carrie to say more or for someone to hand me a bag I could use. When I encountered the pungent odor of hydrogen peroxide, I spun around. Heck with heaving, I was going to pass out realizing how close I may have been to becoming another body in the dump. Judy handed me a damp cloth for my face and a cold soft drink.

"Ben, this no place to practice your pickup lines. Get on with it so we can get out of here before Lily loses her dinner or does something equally theatrical." Dahlia harrumphed. The room went quiet as I faced Dahlia, squared my shoulders, and dropped my hands to my side like a gunfighter about to draw.

"Don't worry, Dahlia, I'll save the theatrics for opening night. I have a venue in which to do my grandstanding, so I don't have to act like a drama queen when I've barged into someone's home. Surely, you must have a better place than my kitchen to play bad cop." Austin squelched a smile before Dahlia could catch it.

"Ooh, that's a good line. Are you getting all this, Julie?" Zelda asked.

"How could I miss it?"

"Let's all take a breath and calm down," Austin pleaded. "We're tired and horrified by what we've witnessed out there. Before you two challenge each other to mud-wrestling in the slime pit, let's end this." Zelda's head whipped around to catch Julie's eye.

"I've got it. Mudwrestling. Slime pit," Julie said and then she yawned. "Another rewrite coming up, but we've already got three dead bodies in the slime pit. We don't need anymore!"

"Three? Where'd you get that? I count four, so far," Ben commented. A silence fell upon us. "And, I might add, our night is far from over."

"That's true, but for now, get a bite print from Marlowe, okay?" Austin asked Ben. "Since the Sheriff's Department asked for our assistance, Rikki's going to be here shortly. She'd like to send out an alert with a copy of that print ASAP. If some guy turns up in an ER with a dog bite, the doctors can use the print to see if it's a match."

"Will do. If someone can help me with the wee doggie, I can swab and print him, and then we can, indeed, get out of here."

"Marlowe trusts me," Julie said, yawning again. "I'll hold him so his momma, and everyone else can go clean up."

"Thanks, Julie." I said as Judy handed me the homemade goop that I prayed would get rid of the stench.

"Don't leave it on your hair too long, or you'll come out of this a blond," Zelda warned. I nodded and tried to make my escape when Dahlia opened her mouth again.

"Wait a second, Bag Lady." I stopped so fast, my plastic-covered feet squeaked on the tile floor.

"Oh, no, you did not just say that, did you, Police Lady? Not after the hunky good cop told you to play nice." My petite, hot-headed friend had balled up her hands into fists. The heck with mudwrestling in the slime pit. Zelda was preparing for a takedown right here and now. I'd make it a tag team event, except that I was too tired to drag this out any longer.

"It's okay, Zelda. I can handle the Police Lady." In that instant, I'd figured out exactly how to fix Dahlia's wagon. It had finally dawned on me who Aunt Lettie had been speaking to the night I overhead part of her telephone conversation about Penney Lincoln. The man on the phone with her was still around, and he could cause trouble for Dahlia if I complained to him. "The rest of you can leave for a soak in a tub or a shower after busting your behinds to save the theater building."

"Thank goodness," Melody said, hugging Darjeeling as she and Carrie left the kitchen. Zelda shuffled off more slowly, staring over her shoulder at Dahlia, as she remained a few steps behind them. Even after they were out of sight, I could tell they were in the hallway listening.

"Ben, get the evidence you need from Marlowe so you can go back to doing police work without being chewed out because your boss is annoyed with me." He nodded and very efficiently swabbed Marlowe's teeth and gums and took an imprint of his bite.

"Austin, thank you for your help. I hope when Rikki gets here, instead of being a heartless shrew, she'll suggest you go home, take a shower, and get some sleep."

"As for you, Dahlia—I'll keep it simple. Go."

"Look that Bag Lady comment was unnecessary, Lily."

"Ignorant and insensitive, too," Zelda said in a voice that carried from where she stood in the hall.

"I admit it could have sounded like that," Dahlia replied, "although I meant it in a teasing way." My friends responded with a chorus of harrumphs as Ben packed up and headed for the backdoor, taking that orange bag with him. As soon as he stepped outside, Dahlia continued.

"I'm creeped out by the idea that a serial killer is on the loose, and that he's killed people I know—or think I know. Not just Penney Lincoln, but, off the record, I'm almost certain his latest victim is a woman who works at the school my brother's kids attend."

I nodded in response to what Dahlia had just said. I could understand. I sighed and spoke in a more conciliatory manner.

"This has been hard for us all, Dahlia. I'm running on empty, and I've got a short fuse. Can we say goodnight and start over tomorrow? I don't really want to answer questions or dwell on the fact that a psycho serial killer was inches away from me before Marlowe ran him off."

"It's a deal. That's what I was going to suggest when I stopped you. I apologize for doing it in a nasty way. Let's talk in the morning."

"Sure, we'll have coffee waiting," I said as she shuffled out the door. When the door shut behind her, it's as if the oxygen had returned to the room and I could breathe again.

"Judy, do you want me to drive you home?" Austin asked, knowing full well she was still in earshot.

"Nah, sweetie," Judy said as she stepped back into the kitchen from around the corner in the hallway. "I planned to stay overnight so we could work late on the play and get an early start again tomorrow. There's no reason for you to drive all the way home either. I can bunk with Lily, and you take Lettie's suite." Then she looked at me.

"It's not safe, is it, Lily? You tell him."

"No, it's not. Judy's right. Whenever Rikki gets here, if she doesn't send you on an assignment as far away from this place as she can, grab your 'go bag' and come on back. You've got a key and the security code, so let yourself in and make yourself comfortable."

"Thanks. I'm too exhausted to argue. You sure must have confidence in that potion you made for Lily if you're going to share her room." He smiled at Judy. Even with a weary, dirty face, his smile can lift me right out of my shoes—when I'm wearing them. "Rikki definitely needs me on this. I'll fill you both in tomorrow."

"Me too!" I shook my head as Zelda waltzed back into the room. "We gotta figure out what we're up against to get our play ready. What's a 'go bag?'"

"You can't leave me out, either—I'm the writer, remember?" Julie added as she stepped into the room. Little Marlowe, who'd fallen asleep in her arms, yawned. Our writer answered Zelda's question. "A 'go bag' is a pack of essentials guys like Austin keep with them since they never know when they're going to have to run for it."

"Like underwear and a clean shirt?" Zelda asked.

"Yeah. A gun, cash, and a passport too, maybe," Julie added as Marlowe woofed. "He gets it."

Melody and Carrie had also come back into the kitchen. They just stood there with steely gazes fixed on Austin, not saying a word. Austin held up both hands in surrender.

"I know when I'm outnumbered. Have it your way—breakfast and an update from the slime pit. Yum!" He glanced at his phone as it pinged almost in sync with a knock on the door. "Rikki's here."

"What do you mean 'here?'" I asked. Too late. Austin opened the door and Rikki walked in. She wrinkled her nose at the lingering *Eau du Decomp*. Then she caught sight of me.

"A homemade hazmat suit—put into use after the fact, so I've been told. It's creative, I'll give you that." Rikki was wearing the real deal. "You should crack some windows to get a cross-breeze and clear the air in here."

I stood there, not sure how to respond in my mortified state. It didn't matter because Rikki wasn't done talking. The consummate professional, her demeanor was serious without being officious. There wasn't a hint of derision or disdain in her manner. In fact, she paid us a compliment.

"You all have handled this situation remarkably well. I'm not just talking about Austin, either, although it's lucky for us that he was here. I'm going to sit in when you give your statements to Dahlia in the morning if that's okay with you."

"Of course," I said. What else could I say? I felt less like a jinx after hearing her comment about Austin's presence being lucky.

"It's gonna be a full house," Judy muttered as she opened the window above the sink about an inch.

"We'll set up in the dining room," I replied with a pasted smile on my face. "See you around eight if that's okay."

"That's great. Don't knock yourself out. Good strong coffee will keep us going," she said before turning to Austin.

"I need to debrief with you, then you can clear out. I'd like you to join Dahlia and me in the morning. Once she gets everyone's statements, we can figure out who's going to do what. There's a ton of work to be done with four murders to investigate." She dropped her voice as she finished the sentence.

"Sit down and talk in here where it's dry. None of us has had a chance to get cleaned up, so we'll leave you alone. Help yourselves to water or a cold drink from the fridge." The others filed out as I said that. "I'm going to excuse myself. Good to see you, Rikki," I said with as much dignity as I could muster wearing garbage bags and stinking to high heaven. Judy handed me another trash bag to dispose of my Slimy Chic outfit. Bag Lady was about right.

∞ ∞ ∞

I HAD TO shower three times before I felt clean enough to go to bed. I'd poured all sorts of shampoos and conditioners into my hair. After using the skunk odor remover, I needed something to get rid of the smell it left on my hair. By the time I finished getting cleaned up and put on the softest pair of pajamas I own, Judy was out cold.

I slipped through the French doors leading out onto the balcony. The rain had all but stopped, and the moon peeked through the clouds. My suite is on the second floor of the sprawling Santa Barbara style house. I have a great view from here of the entire vineyard, the theater surrounded by trees, and the winery across the road. When the clouds parted, the full moon made some of those features visible.

Tonight, the lights around the theater were on. I could see the tented area set up around the slime pit. The tent was lit up, too, casting eerie bluish tinged light. As the crime scene investigators carried out their gruesome duties, shadows and shapes moved.

Beyond that, I could see the fence and woods near where the tree had burst into flame, revealing the man with the virulent gaze. Those woods had been a fairyland in which my friends and I spun tales of enchantment, built a clubhouse, and camped out. Technically, as a preserve area, it was off limits to us, but it felt like our secret garden. I never remember ever seeing anything but beauty during our explorations. How old were those bones? Had we walked over the graves of the unfortunate souls buried out there?

With people in hazmat suits coming and going from the brightly lit tented area, it looked more like a scene from a sci fi movie. One of those b-movies in which the saucers had landed and authorities are hauling the aliens into tents to dissect them. I'd slithered around in a form-fitting scaly skin as a lizard-lady with a tiny part in such a movie. "I mean you no harm," had been my only line. Not something that wild-eyed demon could say to me or anyone else.

I tried to remember what I could about Penney Lincoln. A strawberry blond with a pretty smile when she wore it. She'd been moody—funny at times, but mostly sullen and standoffish. Penney had an odd mix of friends, not that I knew her or anyone else well.

Nor do I have any room to talk about Penney's moodiness. That was my first year in middle school in a place where my southern accent stood out like a sore thumb, and most of my classmates had grown up together. I was still stinging from the fact that my mother and stepfather had sent me to live with Aunt Lettie to get rid of me. It was too soon to know that it was the best thing my parents could have ever done for me.

"I miss you Aunt Lettie," I whispered to the breeze as a cloud floated in front of the moon. I held my breath as I heard movement below. A pebble hit the rail of the balcony and I stepped back. Then a hail of gravel pinged off the wrought iron railing.

"Lily!"

"Austin?" I asked in a hoarse whisper as I leaned over the rail.

"Yes. Please, let me in. I'm locked out."

"Where's your key?" He stood too far away for the porchlight for me see him clearly.

"I'm not sure. I left it inside somewhere." The moon reappeared, and I could see he was barefoot and wearing nothing but a pair of pajama bottoms. His pleading caused my heart to do a little flip-flop. "Mercy, please? Come downstairs and let me in. I need to sleep before I've got to face Rikki and Dahlia and your entire posse. I'll meet you at the front door, okay?"

"Oh, all right. I'll be right down." I wasn't completely convinced this wasn't a ploy. I'd met a few "players" in Hollywood who had come up with outrageous angles to ensure we ended up alone in the middle of the night. I'd never met a guy like that who would have put up with what I'd already asked of Austin.

Maybe if he hadn't been sent away for two weeks on an assignment soon after we'd met, I'd be more willing to take a chance on love. When he left, it had hit me hard that Austin has a dangerous job that would take him away from me on a regular basis. Would men be shooting at him the way they had done when we met? Austin had tried to reassure me that most of the time fugitives didn't fire a single shot. Often, the culprit was already in custody and Austin's role was prisoner transport.

It was so soon after burying Aunt Lettie, though, that I'd lost my nerve. It suddenly seemed too risky to become seriously involved with a man I could lose at any minute. I peeked over my shoulder at Judy resting so peacefully. Her words came back to me.

"Who are you kidding? You can't turn off the sparkle you get in your eyes when he walks into the room or smiles at you."

"I can try," I'd said. Judy was doing her best to step in for Aunt Lettie—bless her heart.

I quietly opened my bedroom door and closed it behind me. Not completely. I never do that now, or Marlowe drives me nuts. With all the extra people in the house, one or more of my pals get up almost every night for a drink, to find something to eat, or just to use the bathroom, and Marlowe's off to play detective! Maybe I should have chosen another name for him.

I hope my pintsized watchdog settles down at some point, but for now, he's on security duty twenty-four-seven. When I got downstairs, there he was standing on his hind legs, peeking out of the window next to the front door. He ran to the door, stood up, and pawed at it, before returning to the window. His stubby tail wiggled so hard, he appeared to be doing a little dance. At least he wasn't barking.

"Get in here," I whispered to Austin, holding the door open.

"Gladly!" Austin practically jumped inside. As he did that, he brushed against me. His skin was cold.

"Come with me," I ordered him. "What were you doing out there?" I asked as I took him to the reading room that had been Lettie's study while I grew up here.

"I thought I heard someone outside. When I ran out to check, I didn't mean to latch the door, but when I tried to get back in, it was locked."

I picked up a throw and wrapped it around Austin's shoulders. I was so close I could smell the fresh air in his hair and on his skin. The fragrance of the Sandalwood soap he'd used made me dizzy.

"I'm so glad you're okay after what went on out there," he whispered, pulling me close. "I never should have left you alone—not even for a minute. I don't know what I'd do if I lost you." I luxuriated in the comfort of his arms.

"I feel the same way, Austin. I just need a little more time." For the life of me, with my head on his chest, I couldn't fathom why. There must be a million ways to lose the man you love—no matter what his profession. In fact, since we'd met, I'd come closer to being killed than he had.

"Take all the time you need. Just don't push me out of your life while you're making up your mind."

"I won't," I said as I reached up, put my arms around his neck, and kissed him. We were lost in that kiss when I heard toenails clicking on the wood floors in the hallway—two sets of them. Marlowe and Darjeeling bolted into the reading room.

"Darjeeling, you come back here right…" Melody

stopped in the doorway. I was about to say something, thinking we'd startled her. Both dogs growled and barked, as Melody pointed and screamed.

5

The Numbers Man

BEFORE I COULD figure out what Melody was pointing at, she swayed. She was going down! I ran to catch her. Austin, still in his bare feet, grabbed a poker from the fireplace and took off.

"Call 911. I don't know if there are still uniformed officers on the property or not! Call Jesse, too!" I covered Melody with the throw Austin had dropped on the floor. As I grabbed the phone in the room and dialed 911, I heard footsteps upstairs.

"Who's there?" Zelda hollered as the front door slammed.

"In here!" I yelled waiting for a dispatcher to pick up. Zelda came into the room and almost tripped over Melody.

"Ow! You kicked me!" Melody yelped as she struggled to sit up, all twisted up in the throw. When Zelda stopped abruptly, Judy and Julie collided with her.

"Judy, use the second line in the kitchen. Call Jesse and tell him to get up here to the house now!" Judy didn't hesitate. I gave Melody a little shove so she could sit up as

Carrie knelt beside us.

"What's happened? Are you hurt?" Carrie asked.

"No. Just scared witless one too many times tonight. Is it still tonight?" Melody asked.

"Yes, barely," Zelda replied. She had a wicked-looking stiletto-heeled shoe in her hand. I had no doubt she could have wielded it effectively as a weapon—unless an intruder was armed with a gun. "Will you tell us what's going on? Why is Judy calling Jesse?"

"Hold on for a second. I'm waiting for the dispatcher to finish her 'what is the nature of your emergency' question."

"This is Lillian Callahan. We have an intruder at The Calla Lily Vineyards. Deputy U.S. Marshal Austin Jennings is after him—on foot."

"Another one?" she asked in an incredulous tone.

"Yes, another one, or maybe the same one again. Are there any officers still on the property?"

"Let me check." In seconds, she was back. "Yes. They're on their way. Would you like me to remain on the line with you until they arrive?"

"No, I..." I stopped speaking when I heard pounding on the backdoor. "They're here now. Thanks!" As I hung up the phone, I heard men's voices as they stormed into the kitchen after Judy opened the door. Jesse and two of his men came rushing into the reading room.

"Everyone okay?" he asked. Carrie was wearing shorty pajamas and had her hair up in twisty bows. Jesse smiled.

"We're fine," Carrie replied, returning Jesse's goofy smile with one of her own.

"No, we're not!" Melody interrupted and whacked

Carrie on the arm. "A man was looking in the window. Austin went after him, half-dressed." All eyes were on me. Before I could say a word, a gunshot rang out from behind the house. The shot was followed by a cry.

"Austin!" I said and took off through the kitchen. I ran out the back door in my pajamas and a pair of black velvet slippers that slid on the wet grass. I regained my balance, kicked off the slippers, and ran barefoot. Marlowe was ahead of me and dashed through the small parking lot where a lamppost gave off a low light.

"Austin!" I yelled as loud as I could as I kept running across the greenspace toward the fence.

"Here!" he responded. "I could use a little help." I heard another cry of pain as Jesse and his men blew past me as if I was standing still. By the time I caught up with them, two police officers were on my heels and the divas were closing fast.

The scene we encountered was a bizarre one. A gun lay on the ground in a pool of light as one of Jesse's men held a flashlight on it. Austin was bleeding and Ben, in the hazmat suit, was examining Austin's wound.

"Should you be doing that?" I asked. "What if you transfer something nasty from the slime pit to him?"

"I'm back on duty after a two-hour break." He did a double-take when he realized who I was. "Wow, you're gorgeous when you aren't dressed head to toe in plastic bags. Why do you look familiar to me too?" I wasn't sure what to say. Under the circumstances this didn't seem to be the time or place to discuss my soap opera career.

"Never mind. Anyway, I'm fresh as a daisy since I just suited up and was heading to the tented area when that young man hanging on the fence almost knocked me down. He probably wasn't sure where he was after Austin wrestled a gun away from the little fool. That could also explain how he chose an eight-foot, barbed-wire fence as his escape route."

"It wasn't this tall before or as sharp. Get me down," the boy groused in a sulky voice. The plump freckle-faced teen was in quite a fix. When he'd tried to scale the fence, his clothes had become tangled on the barbed wire. I was thankful I'd declined the option to install razor wire when we'd redone the fence to improve security. That stuff can kill an intruder.

"As you said, Austin, nothing but a graze. I should be getting back to work now that you have help," Ben said and took his leave with a few last words for the "little fool."

"You picked the wrong night to sneak around here! Consider yourself fortunate that you didn't get shot. These gentlemen don't miss." In the hazmat suit, Ben almost looked like a spaceman in the moonlight as he slowly made his way toward the tent in the woods. The kid on the fence didn't say a word.

"David and I are going to try to lift you up and away from the fence while Marco, here, cuts the wire," Jesse said, taking charge. "Don't fight us, understand? If you do and we let you slip, something you value might get snipped. Got it?"

"Yes! Just get me down, please! Don't let that guy in the pajamas kill me, okay?" Jesse tried not to laugh as he spoke.

"Who? Deputy U.S. Marshal Austin Jennings? He's not

going to kill you. He wants to put you in lock up with lots of big guys like me. That's what happens when you shoot a police officer."

"I didn't know he was a police officer. I thought he was working with the Numbers Man."

"Billie Dundee, is that you?" Judy asked.

"Yes, Judy. Please don't let them kill me or put me in lockup." Then he started to sob as his tough guy demeanor dissolved into those tears.

"Be quiet and hold still," Jesse ordered in a softer tone. In two minutes, they'd cut him loose and had him on the ground. Pieces of his pants still hung on the fence, where Marco had cut them off below the knees to set him free. One of the police officers had run to his car parked in front of the house and returned with a first aid kit. He'd already cleaned and bandaged Austin's arm and went to work on Billie. When he raised Billie's shirt, we gasped at the dark, ugly bruises on his chest.

"How'd you get those?" The officer asked Billie as he examined him while a fellow officer bathed them both in light.

"Fell off my bike." I didn't see skinned knees or elbows like those I'd received when I fell off my bike or roller skates. There was another bruise just above the knee.

"You need to be more careful," the officer warned as he dabbed at Billie's scratches from the barbed wire.

"Ouch! That stings!" Billie bellowed. Marlowe had leaned in to get a closer look at what was going on. When Billie hollered, Marlowe turned around a leaped into my arms.

"Stop griping. Now that you're a bigtime prowler

armed with a gun, pain is going to be a way of life." Then the officer turned to us.

"He's going to need a tetanus shot if he hasn't had one recently, but no stitches. Maybe some ice where he took it on the chin playing cop killer. Do you want us to take him to the station, charge him, and call his parents?"

"No, that's not necessary," Austin replied in an officious manner. "I believe we can let him off with a warning this time. Confiscate the weapon, though, and take it with you, please."

"Thanks, Jesse, for coming to the rescue," Austin said. "Can you post someone at the gate to let his parents in when they get here?"

"Will do," he said. "I'll see you all tomorrow—uh later today, I should say."

"Judy, can you call Billie's parents?" Austin asked.

"You bet I can," she replied, although she didn't look happy about it. "Jim, let's get him up on his feet so we can all go indoors and get them on the phone." Austin stepped in and he and the officer Judy addressed as Jim almost picked Billie up from the ground. He continued to wail as they set him on his feet and then smacked his forehead.

"Officer, please arrest me. That's my dad's gun. I'm safer in jail because he's going to kill me when he finds out I took it and it's confinscated." I tried not to laugh at the audacious kid who couldn't be more than twelve or thirteen.

"Confiscated," Julie corrected him. Our writer had joined us.

"Yeah, that's what I said. That's what's going to get me killed."

"Your dad can get it back if he shows proof of ownership," Jim responded as he prepared to leave. "He's going to pay a stiff fine, though, for not keeping it locked up properly."

"I'll pay for it. How much will it be?"

"A thousand bucks, at least, if your dad doesn't want jail time," he snapped.

"Oh, no. Heck with jail—just shoot me!" Then he glanced at Austin, standing there with his arms crossed. "Never mind. I didn't mean it."

"Billie, no one's going to hurt you. I'm Lily Callahan. I live here, and I'd like to ask you something."

"I know who you are. I saw you with Lettie before, but she's dead, so now you're the owner of the vineyard. Everyone says no spoiled Hollywood actress can do what Lettie did around here." He shrugged. "What do you want to know?"

"Why did you come here so late at night, carrying a loaded gun, and why were you staring into my window?"

"I figured the Numbers Man would be here tonight, and I wanted to take a picture of him."

"How were you going to do that, smarty pants?" Zelda asked as we walked back to the house. Julie must have turned all the lights on in the house in addition to the light on the deck.

"That's a no-brainer—I'm a smarty pants with a smarty phone," Billie snickered as he pulled a cellphone from a pocket.

"In case you hadn't figured it out, to take a picture at night you need a flash. Does that mean the Numbers Man was meeting you for a photo op?" Zelda asked with a skeptical expression on her face.

"Are you kidding? No way! He walks around in the woods talking to himself, counting rocks and sticks, and laying them out in circles or squares. Then he messes them up, angry and crying, and stomping around—it's scary."

"So, when your camera flash went off, what was your plan, genius? To shoot him?" Melody asked cuddling Darjeeling.

"No. That's premeditating, right? You're not going to get me on that because I only brought the gun for self-defense. I wanted the flash to surprise him, so he'd turn around, and I'd get a good picture. Then I figured I could outrun an old guy like that."

"Unless he carries a gun for self-defense too," Carrie suggested. "You're a headline waiting to happen, aren't you Billie Dundee?"

"Don't sweat it. I know who you are. You're the reporter for the Angels. Your team sucks." Carrie sniffed and then shrugged. She'd said almost the same thing to us when she'd decided to take all her unused vacation days and stick around rather than go back for the rest of baseball season.

"Why tonight?" I asked as we stepped up onto the deck. Judy rushed into the house, with most of my friends following her.

"I already told you. I knew he was going to be here."

"How?" Julie asked.

"Because I figured out that his counting was running backward—like a NASA countdown, you know? He was at zero tonight for blast off! I was right about him being here, wasn't I?" Billie asked as we stepped into the kitchen. "I saw him sneaking around. I thought you came outside to meet him, Marshal, where he was waiting in the parking lot."

"Where?" Austin asked as he gazed out the kitchen door. Billie turned and pointed.

"Behind the truck, see?" That truck wasn't usually in the lot. I hadn't seen it arrive, but there was a large reel of coated wire in the back. It must belong to someone who'd hauled in equipment like the tents or lighting.

"Got it." Austin shut the door. Then he stopped and put on his flannel lined jacket that Judy handed him. He'd hung it in the foyer closet when he arrived hours ago so she must have run to get it for him.

"Thanks, Judy." Austin gave her a kiss on the cheek.

"Why did you think he was waiting for me?" Austin asked Billie as he slipped on that jacket.

"Well, he was angrier than I ever saw him before—saying how it was all messed up. He sneaked around to the front of the house and when he saw you, he stopped spitting and hitting himself, so I figured he was looking for you. Or maybe it was when Lily came out on the balcony." Billie paused to think about it. "Sorry, I can't remember for sure. Thanks to you I lost him. I watched you go into the house and when I turned around, he was gone. I decided to check what was going on in the tent that's set up in the woods. Then I thought maybe the Numbers Man went back around to the back and you let him inside. When a light went on, I hoped I still had a chance to snap a picture of him through the window."

"Well, you scared me nearly to death," Melody crabbed at him.

"I'm sorry. I didn't mean to, and you scared me back! I was still looking around the room for the Numbers Man when you screamed. I tore off. How was I supposed to know a cop was chasing me and not the Numbers Man? Besides, what kind of a cop comes after a kid with a fireplace tool wearing and almost no clothes?"

"The kind of cop who sees a peeping tom trespassing in the middle of the night, within a few hundred yards of a crime scene. Did you see what the Numbers Man was wearing?" Austin asked.

"Yes. The same thing he always wears. A sweatshirt with a hood, a camo jacket with a zipper, and pants stuck into his boots." I caught Judy's eye and she nodded. "The first time I saw him, I figured he was a hunter."

"I'm pretty sure we saw him earlier tonight while it was still storming," Judy informed him.

"I didn't count on the storm being so bad. It slowed me down, which is one reason I got here so late. I stopped at the Hayward's barn to wait for it to blow over. I guess the Numbers Man didn't care about a storm."

"When you say he's old—do you mean old like me or old like your mom and dad?" Judy asked from where she was on the phone calling Billie's parents.

"I don't know for sure. He was always out after dark, and the hood hides his face. I don't even know if his hair is gray or white or if he's bald. He sounds like an old man." Then he demonstrated what he meant by that. "That's not always how he sounds, though."

"What does that mean?" Melody asked as we all stood around in the kitchen. We were waiting for Billie to answer when Judy interrupted us.

6

Loco Parentis

"Hello, Betty, it's Judy Tucker." Billie buried his face in his arms folded in front of him on the breakfast bar. "I know it's late, but we've got Billie here at Calla Lily Vineyards. Have the police contacted you yet?"

Judy held the phone away from her ear. From what I could hear of Betty Dundee's angry bellow, she was asking, "what has he done now." Not in a polite way, either. Her tirade continued until Judy cut her off.

"Come pick him up, and he can explain it to you, okay? When you get here, just pull up to the gate and Jesse will let you in. Also, Billie's not the only trouble we've had here tonight. If you see police on the property, they're not still hanging around because of him." Judy scowled as she hung up the phone.

"You were going to tell us more about how the Numbers Man sounds," Judy said. She was still trying to compose herself after dealing with Betty Dundee.

"Sometimes he talks squeaky, in a high voice like a girl—then he answers himself in baby talk. But most of the time, it's an old man's voice."

"He's seriously disturbed, so I can understand why he scared you. What I don't understand is why you kept following him."

"It's because he's old and in trouble, that's why. Someone needs to get him. I guess you'll do that now, won't you, Marshal?"

"We're going to try. He knows his way around here better than we do, but at least we know who we're after. I wish you'd tried to get him help instead of doing it yourself," Austin added.

"I did. My mom said I was making it up. I told my teacher, Ms. Wainwright, too. She said she'd do something about it, but then she called my parents. Dad told her it was a lie and not to bother getting the authorities involved. Nothing has changed since the last time the social worker visited. He's got that right. That's when I thought that if I got a picture of the guy, they'd have to believe me. If you have more questions, you'd better ask them quick. I'm not going anywhere except school while I'm in lockup, Dundee family style."

"That won't stop the police if they have more questions," Austin assured him.

"You know what, Billie?" I said. "Lockup's not such a bad idea until we find the man you've been following. You heard what Judy told your mom. You haven't been our only trouble tonight. The Numbers Man may have committed some very bad crimes."

"Like what?" Billie asked with his eyes like saucers.

"We can't tell you more than that right now," Austin said. "I'm sure if you knew where he lived, you'd tell us, wouldn't you?" Austin asked staring directly into Billie's wide eyes. Billie gulped and nodded his head.

"Yes, I would. I tried to follow him, but I lost him in the woods. I got lost, too, so I never did it again."

"Good for you," Zelda said. "For your sake, I hope he wasn't following you."

"If you should happen to see him while you're at school, go to the nearest phone and call me, promise? Don't talk to him, don't follow him, just go where there are lots of adults around and ask to use a phone. Tell them it's an important police matter and to call me at the number on my card."

"I will." He put the card in his shirt pocket. Then he switched it to a pants pocket before returning it to the shirt pocket.

"You can reach Austin even if you don't have the card with you. Call 911 from somewhere safe. Tell the person who answers your call to locate Marshal Austin Jennings."

"Okay, Lily," he said. "You know what I think?"

"What?"

"People who say you're spoiled are just jealous." That comment drew a round of "aws" from all the women in the room—even Zelda.

"How about a glass of milk and a couple of cookies before your mom shows up?" Judy asked. Billie smiled so big that his eyes all but vanished behind his round freckly cheeks. Austin had that "me too" expression on his face.

"We can all use milk and cookies, can't we? Judy and I have been using Aunt Lettie's favorite recipes to bake cookies for the Thanksgiving Harvest Festival. What do we have to feed Billie before he's placed under house arrest?"

I was making light of the situation, but alarms were going off in my head. I didn't want my recent encounters with psycho family members to cloud my judgment about Billie's situation, but he seemed to be in big trouble at home as well as roaming around in the woods.

Judy took one of the boxes we'd put together for the organizers of this fall's Festival to sample. She passed them around while Austin poured glasses of milk. For the next few minutes our mouths were too full to speak as we devoured cookies from Aunt Lettie's heritage as a southerner—crispy pecan praline, molasses spice, and Mississippi mud cookies. A wave of nostalgia hit me as all the happy hours I'd spent in this kitchen with Aunt Lettie rushed in on me. Maybe it was the familiar flavors, the sweet spiciness in the air, or Judy's presence, since she'd often been with us. Or, it could have been my concern about a twelve-year-old freckle-faced boy whose body might have been among the victims of the Numbers Man. Assuming such a wreck of a man could be our stealthy killer.

"You made these?" Billie asked me after he'd washed down another cookie with milk.

"Yes. Aunt Lettie and I used to bake all the time when I was your age."

"Marshal, she's good-looking and can bake A-plus cookies—you'd better put a ring on it." He did a head slide like a hip-hop dancer and set off a round of laughter.

"Look at you! The little man has got some moves!" Zelda said hopping off the barstool and demonstrating a few dance moves of her own.

"How do you have so much energy?" Julie asked as she yawned.

"Sugar rush! I'm headed for a crash any minute now." She stopped abruptly, so I figured that was it. Then, her face lit up.

"Billie, if I offered a dance class, would your friends join—I mean if I taught it with your help?"

"Really?" Zelda nodded. "Sure, they would!" Billie responded with more enthusiastic head moves. His elation was short-lived. The doorbell rang. "You can count on me if I'm not dead."

Judy ran to the door to let the Dundees in. When they entered the kitchen, I smelled booze on someone. I cringed when I saw the set of his father's jaw. Billie was blinking as if he expected to get smacked. His mother scanned the room, taking in the scene in the kitchen. I thought the horrified look on her face had something to do with the pjs we were all wearing. Apparently, that wasn't it.

"You're not rewarding him with cookies, are you? After we've been inconvenienced by having to drive over here in the middle of the night. What is wrong with you permissive Hollywood people?" I figured Zelda would have a few choice words for Mrs. Dundee, but it was Carrie, our ever-so-sweet-and-chatty sports reporter who spoke up.

"How do you like that? You're inconvenienced? He shot a cop with a loaded gun you allowed a twelve-year-old to get his hands on. Let's not talk about the fact that he's out at midnight in a dangerous storm chasing a deranged killer. I hope the police throw the book at both of you. Billie, if you need a foster mom, I'm it, honey!" I winced at the 'deranged killer' words since we'd tried to be more discrete about what we suspected the Numbers Man had done.

"We're all it!" Zelda added. "You call the cop who was here, Marshal, and tell him to use that loco parentis law to do what he has to do." Judy shook her head.

"That's not what in loco parentis means. It…" Judy didn't get to finish her next sentence.

"Zelda is no lawyer, but she's still right! Billie needs someone to keep him safe. Not that I've completely forgiven him for nearly giving me a heart attack with his peeping tom routine," Melody said. Darjeeling yipped enthusiastically, and Marlowe followed suit.

I couldn't tell who was more shocked by what was going on! Billie or his parents. Or me, to be honest. I hadn't realized how much the "little man" in our presence had evoked the maternal instinct in my thirty-something diva friends who'd suddenly become tigresses. Even Julie, often the most reticent among us, expressed concern.

"Austin, why don't you call the police right this minute and tell them to bring a breathalyzer? Billie should not get into a car with them until we're sure someone's sober enough to drive."

"You know what? Keep him! Our lawyer will contact you tomorrow about the indecent situation going on here," Betty responded. I take it that meant she'd finally noticed the pjs.

"Jim Brady, the police officer who was here earlier, took the gun with him, so you're going to need your lawyer. When Jim examined Billie, he also had questions about several nasty-looking bruises on his body," Judy said.

"The kid's a clumsy ox. There's nothing I can do about the fact that he fell down the stairs," Billie's dad said, glaring at us as if we'd wilt at his bullying.

"That's not how he says he got them," I said meeting his glare with defiance.

"So? Billie's a liar! No one has believed his accusations before. Why would they believe him now?" When Mr. Dundee took a step toward where I was sitting at the breakfast bar, Billie erupted into angry tears.

"Don't you touch her!" He yelled and put up his dukes as he stepped in front of me. Austin stood next to him and pulled a badge from his jacket pocket.

"You need to leave. I'm taking Billie into custody until we can get someone from Children's Services involved. If you don't go now, I'll arrest you for trespassing."

"You don't have jurisdiction here, Marshal." This time when he spoke, Mr. Dundee was close enough that I could tell he'd been drinking.

"It's the middle of the night, you're drunk, and you're behaving in a threatening manner. Heck, I can arrest you," I assured him. "If you insist that we get a local pro to do it, I'll call one of the Sheriff's Department officers still on the property. If they arrest you right now, they might even be able to catch Judy's friend, Officer Brady, before he finishes writing his report about Billie and your gun."

"Come on, Ted. Let's go. You don't want to spend the night in jail, do you?" Mrs. Dundee said as she grabbed her husband's arm. For the first time since they'd arrived, she appeared to be worried. He yanked his arm free and took a swing at Austin. In seconds, Austin had him on the ground with his arms pinned behind him.

"Jail, it is," Austin said as he pulled a pair of handcuffs from his jacket. "Ted Dundee, you're under arrest."

"Judy, call Jim Brady, will you?"

"Gladly!" Judy called Jim on his cell phone. While she chatted with the officer, I checked with Billie.

"Are you okay?" He'd stopped crying but he was petrified.

"For now. I don't want to think about what he's going to do when he's out of jail, and I'm back home."

"Does he hurt you and your mom?"

"Sometimes. Mostly, they hurt each other—after they've been drinking. I try to sneak out when they start fighting, but I can't always do it." When I looked up to see if his mother was listening to our conversation, Betty was no longer in the kitchen.

"Jim's on his way. He hadn't left the property yet" Judy said as she ended her call. "I'm going to the front door to let him in."

"Mom left," Billie whispered.

"Left? Is Betty in the hallway with Austin and her husband?" I asked. No one answered. Betty wasn't the only one who'd left. Billie and I were alone.

"She was, but then Mrs. Dundee tore out of here," Melody said as she came back into the kitchen and began cleaning up. Darjeeling was on her heels.

"She didn't get far," Judy said, bustling back into the kitchen to help. "Betty almost crashed into Jim's patrol car. When she tried to scoot around him, he and his partner cut her off. Austin took Ted outside and he's already in the backseat."

"Wifey-wife is also in the backseat," Carrie said as she came in to grab a notepad she'd left in the kitchen. "She refused to take the breathalyzer test, so she gets to ride along to the police station. They're having their car towed."

"Mom told me to always do that if I got caught drinking and driving. By the time you get to the station, you have a better chance of passing the test."

"I'm sorry you know something like that, Billie," Melody's eyes were misty. "Where is this rascal going to sleep tonight?"

"There's a cot in a storage closet upstairs," I suggested. "Why don't I set it up in Aunt Lettie's suite—in her sitting room?"

"Are you okay sharing a suite with Austin for tonight?" I asked.

"Heck, yes," Billie said, slipped from his barstool onto the floor, and threw his arms around me. I was afraid he was about to cry again. Then, Marlowe jumped up on the barstool next to me and began snuffling Billie's ears. Billie stepped back, smiling. "That tickles."

"Here's the best way to handle that," I said, putting Marlowe into his arms. "Carry him upstairs for me, so we can make up a bed for you."

"What's he going to wear? He can't sleep in those dirty clothes." Melody was emphatic.

"We got you covered, little man," Zelda responded. Carrie was with her and wearing a huge smile.

"They might not be the best team in baseball, but they do lots for kids. I always bring kids' gear with me wherever I go. These pants should fit you, Billie. Don't ask me why they call them brawler pants, but they're great for training."

"For me? Are you serious?" Billie bounced up onto his

toes. "I'm sorry I said they suck. I can be a jerk sometimes."

"Who isn't?" Zelda asked.

"Here's a jersey and a sweatshirt to wear with the brawler pants. The t-shirt and a pair of shorts are comfy enough to sleep in until we can get you some real clothes."

"These *are* real clothes!" Billie was practically vibrating with excitement.

"Don't forget the hat!" Zelda reached into the bag, pulled out a baseball cap, and stuck it on Billie's head. "That's perfect!"

"Thank you so much," he said as Carrie and Zelda smooched him. "This is the best night ever, except for getting stuck on the fence. And for shooting at you, Austin. I'm sorry I did that."

"Hey, it's okay," Austin said, as he came back into the kitchen. He gave Billie's hat a tug. Austin smiled, but it was clear as a bell to me that he was upset—really upset. "That hat looks great!"

"He's rooming with you tonight, Austin. Do you want to help me set up a cot for him? Judy can you come with us and show Billie where the soap and towels are in the bathroom."

"Why don't we all turn in for the night?" Judy said. She must have sensed something was up.

"Amen!" Zelda said. "We've got lots to do in the morning. How are you with a paintbrush, Billie?"

"I don't know, but I'm a quick learner." As they headed down the hall, I lingered a moment to turn off the light in the kitchen.

"Are you going to tell me why you're upset?" I asked

Austin as I slid my arm around his waist.

"They found another body—what's left of it after being in the ground for a long time. Lily, it's a little kid."

He pulled me close, and I wrapped both arms around him as we stood there in the doorway of the darkened kitchen. This wasn't my cowboy's first rodeo, as they say. Austin had tracked down many desperados who'd committed unthinkable crimes. He hadn't said it, but apart from exhaustion, what made this situation hit home was a brazen, sassy-mouthed, abandoned boy. Even though that shot grazed Austin's arm, it had hit him squarely in the heart.

"We'll keep him safe," I whispered. *Austin is so much braver than I am about following his heart.*

7

Three Ring Circus

I AWOKE WITH a start. It felt as if I'd only been asleep for fifteen minutes. There was movement in my bedroom. The gauzy voile drapes billowed in a breeze coming in through the French doors. Had I left them open last night?

"Last night, ohhh," I moaned and shoved the pillow over my head. Had Judy opened the French doors? Where was she?

"Judy!"

"Shh! You'll wake everyone!" She came rushing in from the bathroom, already dressed and ready to get to work. Marlowe bounded onto the bed, spun around, and dug at the sheets. Silly dog.

"What time is it?" I asked as I yawned and hugged Marlowe.

"Almost seven. I'm going downstairs to fix a breakfast casserole to feed an army—including our new 'tween' who really put away the cookies last night."

"I'm going to shower—again—and then I'll be down to help. We need to use the huge coffee pot Lettie bought with the B&B guests in mind. I could drink a carafe full by myself."

"Using the big one is a good idea considering we'll have three police officers at the table. I'll make the usual pot. When you come downstairs, you can set up the big one on the sidebar in the dining room."

"Okay." I started to get out of bed when another wave of ugliness hit me, forcing me backward onto the bed. Marlowe pounced on me, knocking the air out of me. "Did your friend, Jim, tell you they found another body?" Judy nodded.

"No details, he just mentioned the count had gone up to five. Murder by the numbers must be easier than dealing with bodies as people." I sat up on the edge of the bed.

"Especially in this case. Austin said the fifth victim is a small child."

"No!" Judy said, sinking down onto the bed beside me. "No wonder Austin was so upset. I thought he was as disgusted as I was with the Dundees. Poor little Billie. I've known his parents all my life. I never liked them much, but I had no clue they were hurting their child."

"How could you have known?" I put my arm around the sturdy woman's shoulders. "From what we heard last night, even after an investigation by the authorities, Billie was left to fend for himself."

"Ted and Betty have blown it now. Letting Billie get his hands on a loaded gun was a big mistake. A DUI for Betty won't help either. Children's Services will have to do something after they see the awful bruises on his body." She shook her head sadly. "I'm so glad Lettie got you out of the trouble you were in, Lily."

"We'll make sure they do the same thing for Billie. He

can stay here while the court rules on his situation—if that's what he wants."

"With five moms and a grandma doting on him, why would he ever want to leave?"

"My evil doppelganger, Andra, once reported a woman for abusing her child. It wasn't true, but she had designs on the woman's husband and wanted him to dump his wife. Anyway, Julie gave us a mini-lecture on child abuse. Abused children often want their parents' love so much, they'll return to even the worst conditions."

"You didn't. You're just doing what you've done with Austin—preparing yourself for rejection and loss. After all the years you spent with Lettie, you still don't believe you're lovable, do you?"

"Aunt Lettie left me too."

"That wasn't her choice, and it wasn't because she didn't love you." She patted my arm and stood up. "Billie is a smart kid and, the truth is, he's been on his own for a long time. He won't ask to go home. Besides, with both parents in jail, there's no home to go back to for now. In case you hadn't noticed, Austin's not going anywhere either."

"Except off on one dangerous assignment after another, chasing creepy people like the guy skulking around here," I griped.

"There you go! Austin's facing risks right here in your backyard. You and Billie didn't even have to leave home to be in danger and look at what happened to Lettie. Life's hard, and risk goes with the territory. At least Austin's trained to handle it."

"You sound like my therapist. Losing Aunt Lettie, the

way we did, was a setback. It's too bad that's also how I happened to meet Austin."

"First of all, I'd say Austin is an example of how good can come from even a very bad situation. Lettie is still looking out for you, and she doesn't want you to be alone. Second, all this ruminating is a bunch of hooey. If you weren't sure he was a 'keeper,' you would already have told him to get lost."

"Maybe it's me I don't trust. My attraction to him was instant. What if that's all there is to it?"

"Oh, come on. You spent more than a decade in Hollywood where handsome hunks are a dime a dozen. How many of them managed to razzle-dazzle you?"

"Zero." I stood up and stretched. "Thanks for the straight talk. I wish we had a video game machine to distract Billie while we talk to Dahlia and Rikki about last night. He's already heard more than enough for a kid his age."

"I'll help. You and the divas can take turns keeping him occupied."

"I'll let him use my laptop if he promises not to optimize my settings or anything like that. Dahlia and Rikki will want to hear his story about the Numbers Man. Billie could turn out to be a key witness if the guy he's been following around is the killer."

"You don't believe he is?" Judy asked.

"The way Billie described him, the Numbers Man is so disturbed, and his behavior is so odd, he's bound to stand out wherever he goes. How could someone like him have gotten away with murder for so long unless he has an accomplice?"

"I get it. A friend or family member has been keeping the Numbers Man fed, clothed, and sheltered. That doesn't mean they've helped him commit murder." Judy shuddered. "He gives me the willies."

"Me, too. I'll shut up and get dressed so I can help, but here's another question for you. How does a guy that creepy find his victims and coax them into the woods?"

"Are you saying someone does that for him?"

"Maybe," I responded. "If the friend or family member who takes care of the Numbers Man appears to be normal, and Penney Lincoln thought that's who she was meeting in the woods, that could explain how she ended up there."

"Ooh, now I'm really done talking about this. You can never tell what goes on behind your neighbors' doors, can you?"

"No, you can't. Look at Billie. I hope Children's Services sends someone soon, so we can figure out what to do for him next. In fact, we'd better wait until a representative gets here before Dahlia and Rikki interview him."

"You're right. It's going to be a three-ring circus today, isn't it?" Judy asked.

"Tell me about it. We also have the little matter of a three-act play to prepare, which is intended to be a comedy, but not quite a circus."

"Marlowe, are you ready for breakfast or do you want to wait for the ringmaster to drag her behind downstairs?"

"I'll be right down." Too late. Marlowe leaped from the foot of the bed to the doorway in a single bound, performing the first circus act of the day.

8

AWOL

By the time I arrived in the kitchen, Judy had it sparkling. She also had the casserole in the oven. The aroma was amazing, but I zeroed in on the coffee. I drained the first cup and poured another. I took the second cup with me to set up the thirty-cup coffeemaker. Once the coffee was going, I arranged napkins, plates, and silverware for our guests to serve themselves.

I tossed back the last of my second cup of coffee and hustled into the kitchen just as Austin walked in. When our eyes met, he smiled, and my heart did a little flip-flop. More rested and less stressed out than he had been last night, he still appeared a bit nervous. Maybe he wasn't looking forward to discussing murder over breakfast any more than I was.

"You're up early, Marshal," Judy said. Austin swooped her up in his arms and kissed her on both cheeks.

"I woke up worried you'd be down here cleaning and cooking. This house is bursting at the seams and company is coming. You work too hard." He held Judy a moment longer before heading my way. "What is it that smells so good?"

"French toast breakfast casserole. It tastes even better than it smells," Judy said.

"I'll bet they miss you back at the ranch where breakfast can't be as good without you."

"Since my great-nephew and his wife moved in, I hardly have anything to do. He's got all these modern ideas from ag school about how to run a ranch. I don't want to interfere since he's got a good head on his shoulders. They're still in that newlywed 'playing house' phase, too, so both Nicky and Maryann need time to make themselves at home."

"It was nice of you to take them in," I said as I handed Austin a cup of coffee.

"Their decision to come back to Napa Valley after his graduation worked out perfectly since I was seriously considering selling the ranch. I prefer to keep the property in the family. After losing two of my oldest ranch hands in the last year and a half, I'm too tired to start over and train new people to do it my way, but I also know I can't do it myself. Anyway, I already called and told them I'm staying here a couple more days since we're running so far behind."

"Well, I'm glad you're willing to stay put after last night. We might need you around here a little too much." Judy hugged me.

"That could never happen!" Then I got the Austin good morning treatment, too. I was giggling when our newest houseguest sauntered into the kitchen.

"So, Marshal, I see you took my advice." I turned around to find Billie decked out in his baseball outfit, smiling from ear-to-ear.

"Wow! You look great. What advice?" I asked.

"Not yet," Austin replied.

"Good grief!" He smacked his head as he'd done last night. "Where is it?"

"Here, next to my heart," Austin replied winking at Billie.

"Yes! That's a great start, but hand it over." Austin gave something to Billie. Then, Billie went down on one knee.

"Lily, Austin is the best man I ever met. I already figured that out, and I'm just a kid who hasn't even known him for twenty-four hours yet. He should have the best woman I ever met as his best friend. This is for you—a friendship ring."

"Please wear it. It belonged to my grandmother," Austin added. My hand shook as I held it out, and Austin slipped on the ring. Then we sealed our friendship with a toe-curling kiss. Billie cheered, and so did my diva pals who were standing in the doorway. We whooped it up as the divas took a closer look at the ring, until the doorbell rang.

"What fresh hell is this?" Julie muttered, using a favorite quote from Dorothy Parker. "I'll get it. You keep fraternizing with the law."

"It's not even eight o'clock yet," Judy sputtered just as the timer pinged on the oven. When she opened the oven, we were engulfed in the scent of cinnamon, maple, and vanilla.

Dahlia was at the front door, but by the time Julie brought her into the kitchen, Rikki had come in the back way. She and Austin were immediately engaged in a discussion. The rest of my diva friends and I set out milk and juice, and a platter of the bars and brownies Judy and I had baked for the Thanksgiving Harvest Festival organizers.

I'd managed to herd everyone into the dining room when Jesse showed up at the backdoor with a repair crew. Apparently, no one needed to call for assistance. An electronic device installed during their last inspection had signaled trouble.

"What should we do?" Jesse asked Dahlia.

"You know what areas to avoid. If they can find out what they need to know that way, fine. If not, they'll have to come back in another day or two. Sorry, Lily."

"I understand, Dahlia."

"With everything you have on your plate, do you have time to show them around?" I asked Jesse.

"Yes. Fortunately, we finished picking the grapes that were ready for harvest before the storm. Now that the rain has stopped, I've got hands going row by row, checking on the vines, and cleaning up. We'll have a better idea this afternoon of what to do next in the field. I've already given the police my statement, so I won't be missed here."

"Don't count on it," Carrie said as she brushed past him to take a seat at the dining table. Billie and the other divas were already chowing down. Rikki introduced herself and Billie was delighted.

"Wow! A beautiful lady Marshal as your boss! You know how to live, Austin." Rikki smiled.

"I'm glad to meet you, Billie. I understand you almost put an end to Austin's charmed life."

"Not on purpose!" He was worried until Rikki smiled.

"Gotcha!" Rikki said, and Billie laughed.

"Whew! That was a good one."

"All joking aside, Jesse, I'd like to speak to you and Lily about the incident that occurred years ago. If you can come back in an hour or so, we ought to have taken care of the routine matters."

"Sure, we'll get out of here so you can get to work."

"Coffee, to go?" Judy asked as she offered them throwaway cups of coffee she'd prepared. Then she gave them a small box of pecan pie bars. "Something to go with the coffee."

"Always taking care of everyone, aren't you? Thanks!" Judy stood on her tiptoes and gave Jesse a peck on the cheek. As soon as they were gone, Dahlia guzzled coffee, wolfed down her casserole, and got down to business.

"Rikki and I plan to divide and conquer."

"What?" I asked dreading the thought that we were in for a new round of snide remarks.

"Sorry, that didn't come out right. If you have a couple of other rooms we can commandeer, we have two uniformed officers who can help. One of them will work with me and the other with Rikki so we can get the statements done quickly."

"Of course." As if on cue, two officers walked into the dining room.

"Jesse told us to come on in and head back here. He says there's coffee—and, uh, food."

"No rest for the wicked, huh, Jim?" Judy asked.

"Not given what's been going on here." He spotted Billie as he said that.

"You look better than you did last night, son. That's

great gear you've got on."

"I know. Cool, huh?"

"Help yourselves to coffee and food," I said. "Then sit down wherever there's a seat." It wasn't until they moved that I noticed a woman standing quietly behind them.

"This is Diane Constantine from Children's Services. She's here to speak to you, Billie," Jim added as he piled food on a plate. Austin and I both jumped up.

"Please come with us, Ms. Constantine. I'm Lilian Callahan, and this is Deputy U.S. Marshal Austin Jennings." As she followed Austin, I paused and spoke to Dahlia.

"The reading room and the front parlor ought to work for you. If you can get statements from Zelda, Melody, and Carrie first, they'd like to go check on the theater building."

"What about me? I don't want to stay home and miss all the action," Julie said.

"By that, she's hoping Hazmat Man is still loitering somewhere on the property," Carrie snickered.

"Look who's talking. 'Don't count on it,'" Melody said, repeating the comment Carrie had made to Jesse, and batting her eyes.

"Uh, Julie we do want to get your statement," Dahlia was staring at a list as she made that request. "We understand you weren't at two of the crime scenes, right?" Our visitor from Children's Services raised both eyebrows at the mention of crime scenes."

"That's true." Julie replied.

"Okay, then our interview with you will be quick. Follow me, please." Dahlia got up and took her coffee with her.

"If you'll come with me, Ms. Constantine, where it's more private, I can explain. May I pour you a cup of coffee?" Diane Constantine nodded and relaxed a little.

"Black, please."

"Have a seat, Ms. Constantine," I added and set her coffee down in front of her at a table in the morning room off the kitchen. Billie was behind me.

"Please call me Diane," she said, taking a sip of her coffee.

"Hello, Diane," Billie said, giggling. "How are you?"

"I'm fine, thank you. It's Ms. Constantine to you." He giggled again and covered his mouth with his hand to stop it. Diane Constantine smiled too. "I'll need to speak with you in a few minutes, after I've chatted with Lily and Marshal Jennings."

"Billie, why don't you take Marlowe out in the backyard for a little break?" Judy suggested. "He loves to play fetch. There are toys in a box on the deck."

"Sure!" Billie grabbed the last pecan bar from a tray on the kitchen island and headed for the door. "Marlowe, come!" Billie laughed when he realized Marlowe was already at his feet. Fetch, toy, and out are words my pooch understands well.

"I'll go with him. Darjeeling needs to get out too. Someone come and get me when it's my turn, okay?" Melody grabbed Darjeeling who had already assumed she was invited, and had headed for the door as fast as her tiny legs would carry her.

"I hope you can explain what's going on around here. Jim Brady sent me a report about the incident with Billie Dundee. What's this about other crime scenes?"

"There's been some trouble, ma'am," Austin said adopting his old western lawman persona. "Billie's got himself mixed up in it, although we haven't told him most of what's going on. My colleagues will want to interview him as a witness. Since his parents aren't available, we're hoping you can act on his behalf. From what he's told us, he has important information about a man who may have committed five murders." She went pale.

"Here?"

"Oh, no." I said in a hurry. "Not originally, anyway." I gave her a quick rundown of what we knew about the dumpsite in the preserve area and how Calla Lily Vineyards became involved. I wrapped up my summary of events with the incident involving Billie and the reason he was here last night. I left out the fact that he'd shot Austin, but otherwise it was a concise synopsis of everything we'd been through.

"I'm familiar with Billie's background so it doesn't surprise me to learn that he was roaming around at that hour," Diane said. "We've tried to intervene once or twice after he admitted his dad had hurt him, but Billie has always recanted his story. Once he was branded a liar, it has been more difficult to act on concerns about abuse. I wouldn't be surprised if his truthfulness becomes an issue for him as a witness."

"This time you've got more than his word to go on. He's not only out after midnight but he was carrying a loaded gun. When Billie's father attempted to assault an officer of the law, his mother fled, and nearly hit a police car while behind the wheel of her car, drunk as a skunk." A smile flickered across Diane's face at the vehemently defensive tone I'd adopted.

"You've developed a bond with the boy, haven't you?"

"We all have," Austin replied.

"In your case, Calla Lily, it's not too surprising. I have some familiarity with your background." My head shot up at her use of my nickname. "Not only what your aunt told me about you, but I can read the papers. Your family members give Billie's a run for their money, don't they?" Then she smiled broadly. "Let's hear what Billie has to say. I almost didn't recognize him. No one has ever mentioned he has dimples. Where did those come from?"

"He does have a great smile," I replied, "and a smart mouth to go with it. What happens next?"

"Children's Services will continue our investigation while the police complete theirs. Unless they come up with a bundle of cash, the court will appoint attorneys for mom and dad, and another will be assigned to represent Billie. Jim Brady sent pictures of the awful bruising. I need to take Billie to a doctor to have him examined and get him a tetanus shot. His parents will be charged with reckless endangerment and child abuse, in addition to the firearms charge, and the DUI. Maybe more charges will be brought against them, depending on what we find during a home visit."

"I can take him to the doctor's office. I'm also more than happy to hire a lawyer for him when he needs one. It's more than his parents' abuse that we're concerned about when it comes to his safety."

"Typically, when a child is taken into custody, he's turned over to us while we locate a relative or place him in temporary foster care. We also set up a hearing with his parents within a day or two, but I don't know when that can happen given their circumstances. Your worries about his safety mean something else, too, if Billie's also a witness in a murder investigation. When we've considered custody options for Billie in the past, his parents had burned so many bridges that they couldn't tell us if they had any living family members or not."

"Then why not leave him here until we all have a clearer picture of the situation?" Austin suggested. "I could put him up someplace else too, but he won't be as comfortable as he is here. The security team and the police have the entire place under surveillance, hoping to find the man Billie described to us."

"If you need a court order to make this Billie's temporary foster home, I'm sure Lettie's old friend, Judge Brinkley, will help. Tell him Lily begged you to call. I can do it if you'd prefer since I need to speak to him about another issue." Austin shifted in his chair, a sure signal that he'd gone on alert. I hadn't had a chance to tell him about my decision to talk to Colin Brinkley to ask what he'd told Aunt Lettie years ago about Penney Lincoln's disappearance.

"I know Judge Brinkley. He's handled matters for us before." Diane paused and sipped her coffee. "Will Billie have his own room? What about clothes and getting him to school now that classes have started, or making sure he does his homework and brushes his teeth? Do you really understand what you're getting into?"

"Probably not, but I'm willing to try as hard as I can. I'll take him to urgent care this afternoon to get his shot and an examination. I'll arrange for my physician to follow up on Monday. We'll stop and get him some school clothes on the way home. Will he be allowed to go home and get his schoolbooks or can whoever you send to inspect his home bring them to us?"

"I can have someone pick up his books if he tells me where they are," Diane replied.

"We shared Lettie's suite last night, but he'll have it all to himself. I'm going home, and then I'll be on the road for a couple of days." I drummed my fingers on the table, wondering when he'd planned to share his news with me.

"I give up! Calling Judge Brinkley is a great idea since we're facing a long holiday weekend. I don't know why they start school right before Labor Day. You'll have to postpone the follow up with your physician until later in the week, but at least you'll have an extra day to get Billie situated here. Tuesday morning, you should check-in at the administrative office, then go to class with Billie and introduce yourself to his teacher."

"Ms. Wainwright?"

"No, thank goodness. Lydia Wainwright was Billie's teacher last year in sixth grade. I'll email you the basic information about the school calendar, his course schedule, class times, and teachers. As soon as I get the go-ahead to assign you as his foster parent, I'll fax the authorization to the school. They'll need that to allow you on the school grounds and to grant you permission to speak to his teachers." I tried to pay close attention, but I was distracted by her remark about Lydia Wainwright.

"Thanks. I appreciate your help. Why did you say that about Ms. Wainwright?" I asked.

"All Billie Dundee needs is another unreliable adult in

his life Apparently, she didn't report for duty as expected. No one has been able to locate her, and she hasn't bothered to contact anyone with an explanation."

"Has she been reported as a missing person?" Diane shook her head no in response to Austin's question. That did nothing to settle the growing sense of dread I felt as Diane continued.

"My coworker has a new sixth-grader in her caseload, so she asked a few questions when she was told Ms. Wainwright's students were being moved to other classrooms. Another teacher at the school told her the Vice Principal spoke to Lydia's sister, who insisted there was no reason to worry. She claims Lydia took off to Vegas for a quickie wedding. After that her new husband was taking her on a honeymoon to Hawaii."

"Without telling anyone else?" I was incredulous. "Does she have a history of instability?"

"To be honest, I don't know. What I've just told you is second or third-hand information. I'm sure there are all sorts of stories being told about why Ms. Wainwright is AWOL. I didn't want to you be caught off guard if someone mentioned it since she was Billie's teacher last year."

"Thanks for the head's up. I'm grateful for everything you're doing for Billie. Will you say anything to him about Ms. Wainwright?"

"I will if he brings it up. I'm glad he's in a place where he's welcome, and I've never seen him so happy. I really need to get crackin,' as your Lettie used to say. Do you have any idea when they plan to interview Billie?"

"Let me find out," Austin said, springing into action.

"Can I get you more coffee or would you like me to have Billie come in so you can speak to him?"

"Both, please." She'd pulled out a tablet device and appeared to be making notes or filling out forms. When I came back with fresh coffee, she was still at it. Billie's face was flushed when he sat down.

"Marlowe loves to play. Darjeeling tries hard to keep up, but she's not much bigger than the tennis ball. I've never seen a dog that small. Melody says she's a teacup Yorkie and Darjeeling is the best tea ever grown. Great name, huh?"

"It is," Diane agreed.

"Julie told me Marlowe's named for a detective in books written by a guy named Chandler who wrote about the mean streets of LA."

"Oh yes, Philip Marlowe. He was a character in a wonderful old movie I've watched many times *The Maltese Falcon*," Diane responded.

"Yes, I know. A part played perfectly by a man I never heard of before—Humphy Bogart. No, that's not right—Humphrey Bogart. Melody says it's a classic movie even though it's not in color. She says we'll watch it and she'll show me how you don't need color because of the light and shadow. Can you believe that?"

I was enthralled by Billie's enthusiasm, but I forced myself to step away. After all the coffee I'd had, no way was I going to get through an interview with the police without a stop at the bathroom. When I stepped out into the hallway, I ran into Austin—literally.

"Whoa, slow down there, little lady." I rolled my eyes at Austin's corny comment.

"Give it a rest, lawman, or my posse will come after you for calling me a little lady, which I'm not. I may send them after you anyway for keeping secrets from me."

"Me? When were you going to tell me you remembered who Aunt Lettie's old friend was and planned to call him about Penney Lincoln's disappearance? The Numbers Man already has his eye on you. Why do you want to attract attention by running around town asking a bunch of questions?"

"Do you believe the man Billie described is capable of carrying out surveillance?"

"No, but he doesn't have to be the one doing the surveillance, does he?"

"Does that mean the authorities are considering the possibility that someone other than, or in addition to, the Numbers Man is involved in the murder of Lydia Wainwright?"

"Yes, although officially, no one has even said she's dead. What I don't understand is if there's a tie-in to Billie's story about having told her about the Numbers Man. When Billie gets to that part of his interview, we should ask him where they were at the time and who else was around."

"I agree, although I don't want Billie to feel that by confiding in his teacher, he's responsible for her murder. We need to ask the question in a casual way. Billie said his teacher promised to help, so maybe she went to wrong person for help. Who knows where she was when she called Billie's parents? Someone could have overheard her when she was on the phone with them."

"Yeah, you mean the way an all-too-curious twelve-year-old snooped on her aunt's phone call?"

"I admit I was curious. She was speaking to a man in a sweetie-pie way. Why wouldn't I be concerned about who he was? That's enough about me. Why are you leaving town?" He didn't have a chance to answer.

9

Billie's Bombshells

"THERE YOU ARE!" Judy said. "Billie looks like he's been sent to detention. Get in there and support him. The rest of us are headed to the theater building."

"Don't you want to support him?" I asked.

"We aren't invited. Besides, with the best man and the best woman he's ever met in the room with him, who else does he need?" Judy gave us both a little shove toward the dining room doorway and left.

When Austin and I sat down next to Billie, he let out an enormous sigh. I reached over and patted his hand. It was as cold as ice. The balance in the room seemed to have shifted now that the four of us sat across the table from Rikki, Dahlia, and Jim.

"Billie, do you understand why you're here?" Rikki asked.

"Yes. Lily explained it to me last night. The Numbers Man might have done some really bad things, and you want me to tell you about him."

"That's correct. Take your time, and if you need a break, tell us. Can you start by telling us the first time you saw him?"

"Last summer, when I was in the woods. He was sitting on a rock with his head bowed, like this." He demonstrated what he meant. "I thought he was asleep, and I didn't go any closer because I didn't want to wake him up. Then I heard him counting—by twos that night."

"You mean like two-four-six-eight?" Dahlia asked.

"Yes, only he kept counting and counting. I listened for a while until, off to the side, I heard a stick breaking like when you step on it. He jumped up to see if someone was coming. That's when he started talking like an old man."

"What was he saying?"

"'You're going to get it now, boy.' There was more, but it's hard to remember because I was nervous. I was afraid he was talking to me until he ran off in the other direction. As soon as he did that, I ran all the way home."

"Can you describe him for us?"

"Austin asked me to do that already," Billie said glancing at us as he answered Rikki's question. "Like I told him, it was dark. The man wore a jacket with camouflage material, boots, and a hood on his head that was a dark color. It wasn't part of the jacket. Maybe a sweatshirt like my new Angels' hoodie, only it was gray or black instead of red." Billie glanced at me and I nodded reassuring him that I understood what he was saying.

"That's good. I'd like you to try to go over it again. Start at the beginning and run it like a movie in your mind. Look at where he's sitting and what he's doing. Is it completely dark or is there moonlight? What do you see or hear? Even if it's a small thing it might matter. Is he wearing a ring or a watch or is there a label or tag on his clothes? Is anything lying on the ground around him?" The room went silent for a few moments as Billie did as Rikki asked.

"It's smelled a little smoky, like maybe he had a fire before I got there. The moon was bright when it wasn't behind the clouds. His boots were old and worn out. I don't think there were real shoestrings in them—string, but not regular string, because it was thicker. Oh, yeah, he had a band tied around his arm—a black one. Here," Billie said pointing to his upper arm.

Funerals for police officers or fallen soldiers immediately popped into my head. The funeral director had the option on a list for mourners when I made funeral arrangements for Aunt Lettie.

"Did he always wear it?" Rikki asked.

"No, but I might not have noticed since I didn't remember it until now. That night, when he thought he heard someone coming, he stuck the black band under the rock he was sitting on. His chewing gum, too."

"You mean a pack of gum or are you talking about chewed gum?" I asked.

Can you get DNA from chewing gum? I wondered if they could find the gum he'd spit out. I'm not sure how much DNA mattered. If the Numbers Man was a recluse, no one was likely to have his DNA on file. Not unless he'd been in trouble years ago. Maybe it could be used to tie him to the victims.

"He spit out the gum he was chewing and covered it in the dirt with his boot. Then he put a pack of gum under the rock." Billie turned to Austin.

"The rock I'm talking about is near where the tent is

set up. It's big enough that you can sit on it and there a few other rocks next to it." I saw Jim Brady jot down a note. I'm sure the investigators had been all over the area by now, but they might not have checked under the rocks.

Then Rikki and Dahlia took turns asking him questions trying to get more details. Where exactly was he the first time that he saw the Numbers Man, and what route had he taken to get there. What time was it. How far it was from where the tent was set up and other questions like that.

"Okay, thanks, Billie." Rikki smiled warmly. "Your testimony is very helpful. If you remember anything else tell Lily or Ms. Constantine, okay? Otherwise, we'd like you to keep this between us for now." Billie nodded solemnly. Diane fidgeted in her seat. I hoped she wasn't considering placing Billie elsewhere—like several counties away or in another state.

"When the movie was running in my mind, I kept getting mixed up. It was hard to keep the stuff I'd seen on other nights from slipping in. He carried a pencil stub and a little black book with him in a jacket pocket. I'm not sure what he was writing in it—maybe numbers. On other nights he didn't just count out loud, he put rocks or sticks on the ground and made shapes out of them. Then, he'd mess it all up. Sometimes he was angry when he did that and used curse words—like he did last night. I can't remember for sure when he did that and when he didn't, but it was scary."

"Why did you go back?" Dahlia asked.

"I like it in the woods. It's peaceful and quiet—no one is yelling or stomping around and fighting. Most of the time, there's no one around at night. The next time I went to the woods, he wasn't there. I hoped maybe he'd left—gone somewhere else, but I found numbers on a piece of wood not too far away from the rocks. A piece of charcoal was on the ground, so I figured that's what he used to write the numbers. That's when I decided to call him the Numbers Man."

"Do you remember what numbers you saw?"

"They were kind of wiped off, Lily, but I'm pretty sure there was a five and then a number I couldn't read. After that a nineteen and two more numbers I couldn't read."

"You mean four numbers together like a year—nineteen something-something?" I asked.

"I'm not sure if I thought that then, but another time the numbers looked exactly like a year—1999." A ripple moved around the room as folks shifted in their seats. I tried not to react. Penney Lincoln had vanished that year. Diane appeared puzzled, but everyone else had connected the dots.

"Were there other numbers with it that time?" Dahlia asked.

"There could have been. I can't remember exactly because I was so nervous. I think that was the time he walked right past me, staring at the ground, and counting backward. I froze. After that, I was always jumpy, and tried never to make any noise because he was jumpy too. I scared him away once when I kicked a rock."

"What made you decide to get a picture of him?" Rikki asked.

"After I watched him a few times, I heard him talking in different voices—not just like an old man. Sometimes he talked like a woman. He cried and talked like a baby, too. I could tell he was in big trouble when he called himself a stupid idiot, or other bad names, and punched himself."

"When was that?"

"Earlier this summer. He was almost always angry and upset, which wasn't that bad because it was easier for me to know where he was. It also made it easier for me to follow him when I tried to find out where he lived."

"When you followed him, where did he go?"

"Toward my house and the Hayward's place. Then he took a path in a different direction and disappeared into the woods. The next time, I was waiting for him closer to where he went into the woods from the other path. The woods are thicker there. He blended into the shadows, and he was gone again. The last time I tried to follow him was a couple of weeks ago. He must have spooked a deer and when it came running toward me, I tried to get away fast, and I got lost. It was almost morning by the time I found my way back home, so I decided not to try that again."

"If you were worried about him, why didn't you tell someone so they could help him?"

"Lily already asked me that. I told her that I tried to get Mom and Dad to help. Mom told me to stay out of the woods and Dad told me to mind my own business. Dad said the woods are a good place for a crazy, homeless guy. When I said the police ought to investigate, my dad got it into his head that I made it all up to get attention. I got whooped."

"I'm sorry that happened to you," Dahlia said. Before she could ask her next question, I asked one of my own.

"Who else did you tell?" I was curious to hear what he

had to say now that I knew Ms. Wainwright wasn't his teacher. Billie had a puzzled expression on his face. I braced myself for the bomb that was about to go off.

"I told you that already too, Lily."

"I know, but when you told me you'd asked a teacher to help, I didn't understand you were talking about your sixth-grade teacher. Where were you when you told her about the Numbers Man?"

"Ms. Wainwright was in the hallway by the office at my new school. I was glad to see her, and I asked if she was going to be a middle school teacher now. She said no, and that she was at the school for a meeting."

This time, a jolt rather than a ripple, made its way around the room. Diane squelched a gasp, trying to pass it off as a cough. Billie's smart though, so he knew something was up. His puzzled expression had turned to suspicion.

"That was before classes started, right?" Austin asked. When Billie answered Austin's question, he spoke slowly as if trying to read our reactions to each word.

"Yes—a couple of weeks ago, right after I got lost in the woods tracking the Numbers Man."

"What were you doing at school?" I was glad Dahlia asked that question since Billie hadn't shared that with us.

"That's what Ms. Wainwright wanted to know. I told her I was going to the library to read about what it means when people talk to themselves in different voices. She wanted to know why, and I said I was worried that this old guy in the woods was in bad shape. When I explained about the Numbers Man, Ms. Wainwright promised to help, and told me not to go back there again. By the time I got home she'd called my parents and I got whooped again."

"Was anybody around when you spoke to her?" I asked, which is what I hoped to get from the retelling of his story—could anyone have overheard them?

"Maybe. I wasn't paying attention because I was so surprised to see Ms. Wainwright. There were people in the office when she opened the door and said goodbye to me. Mr. Dees was in there."

"The principal," Diane interjected.

"Yes, and Mr. Dees' secretary, Ms. Anthony. She was standing at the desk, talking to Coach Durst. He came out right after Ms. Wainwright went into the office. Coach asked me if I was going to the gym to practice my skills. When I told him that I was going to the library, he said that was too bad since practice gives you a head start on the season. I wasn't sure what to say, so he left."

"Okay, so you went to the library. Did you speak to anyone about what you were doing?"

"Not at first, Marshal Rikki. I asked the librarian where the section on mental illness was."

"Ms. Hope or Ms. Teaberry?" Diane asked, taking notes.

"The old one with glasses hanging on a chain around her neck."

"That's Gladys Hope," our rep from Children's Services said aloud, as she added the name to her notes. Dahlia did the same.

"You used different words when you asked the librarian your question," I remarked.

"Yes, that's because Ms. Wainwright told me that's

what it means when you talk to yourself. The Numbers Man has a mental illness and I was right that he needed help."

"Did the librarian tell you where to find the books?" Billie nodded and gulped down half a glass of water before answering Dahlia.

"Yes. She walked me over to the shelf. Then she asked if I planned to be a psychiatrist someday. I said no, and that I was worried about an old homeless man in the woods. When I told her where I saw him, she got upset and told me the woods near Calla Lily Vineyards are part of a preserve. Then she asked what was wrong with my parents—didn't they teach me not to talk to strange men? I told her I never talked to him because he talks to himself." I stifled a laugh.

"How did Ms. Hope react to that?"

"She told me homeless men with mental illness are not a child's problem, and I should leave it to the adults."

"I wonder if she or Ms. Wainwright called and reported him to anyone." I looked around the room, but only Diane responded.

"That's a good question. I can check with adult protective services to see if a call came in. It would help to have a more specific date."

"I checked out a few books. They're in my room at home, um, in a box under my bed. The other librarian was there when I left. She put the information into the computer, put a stamp in the books, and told me not to forget to bring them back by then. I guess we should go get them, huh?" He drained the remaining water from his glass and seemed fidgety.

"Billie, would you like to take a break?" I asked.

"Yes, please. I need to use the restroom." As he stood up to leave, he dropped another bomb.

"I'm sorry I can't remember more about the numbers and the dates and stuff the Numbers Man said. If I had my notebook with me, it might help." Dahlia choked on the coffee she was drinking. Rikki pounded her on the back as she spoke.

"Billie, is the notebook under your bed with the library books?" Rikki asked.

"No, after I got into so much trouble with my parents, I stuffed it inside my mattress." Then he asked very politely to be excused—like he was in class. Rikki got up and closed the door after him. Then she checked the door leading into the butler's pantry.

"Do you believe him?" Dahlia's eyes were still running from strangling on her coffee. She managed to croak out those words.

"Believe him about what? Several of us saw someone fitting the description of the Numbers Man here on the property. If what you're asking is, do I believe the guy Billie's been tracking is capable of being your serial killer? I'm dubious. To figure that out, you've got to catch him. One way to validate at least part of what Billie's saying is to get the library books and his notebook," I snapped. Diane spoke up, too.

"There are plenty of people to question—isn't that how you do it? The librarians, the coach, and Billie's parents. My bet's on Gladys Hope as the person most likely to have reported that there was a disturbed homeless man roaming around in the preserve area. The question is—who would Gladys have called? If you don't have a record of a call about him, maybe she called a mental health hotline or contacted a homeless shelter. As I've already offered to do, if you get me the date Billie checked out the library books, I'll see if Adult Protective Services received a report. I'd tell you to ask Ms. Wainwright, but by your reactions, I'd say she's not only missing but dead."

"If you repeat one word of this, I'll charge you with obstructing justice." Dahlia jumped up out of her seat and leaned across the table.

"Sit down, Dahlia," Rikki ordered. "Everyone at this table is on our side. I'm most concerned about the boy."

"Lily, I don't believe Billie should set foot in his house again—not until we've caught the Numbers Man, or maybe never, depending on what Children's Services learns." Rikki addressed Diane next.

"I'd like Jim to accompany you to Billie's house to collect the library books, his notebook, schoolbooks, and whatever else you believe Billie needs while he's away from home. You've relocated children like him before, so you know how to do that efficiently. Plus, you already know what's going on." Diane cut Rikki off.

"Some of what's going on. I don't know how the murder of Lydia Wainwright makes the Numbers Man a serial killer, do I?"

"I stand corrected. You already know some of what's going on—probably more than you should know. For your own safety, I'd keep this completely quiet. As far as anyone is concerned, you're visiting Billie's house because he has no one at home to care for him. I know Lily is willing to offer him temporary foster care here. If you can make that happen, it would be much better than placing him elsewhere, which would involve sharing sensitive information with more people."

"As soon as we're done here, I'll call Judge Brinkley and ask for his help. He's an old friend of Letitia Morgan, so he's already familiar with Lily and the setting in which Billie will be living if he's allowed to remain here," Diane asserted.

"That's good because we briefed Judge Brinkley earlier about the discoveries made here at the vineyard and in the nearby woods. You won't have to explain any of that to him."

"That is good, because I couldn't do it without sounding like a babbling idiot, could I?" Diane paused and poured herself more water from a jug in the middle of the table.

Austin and I exchanged glances. I assumed Colin Brinkley had been briefed because of his involvement, two decades earlier, in the disappearance of Penney Lincoln. He was a lawyer then, not a judge, so I wondered what role he'd played.

"I'm sorry to be snippy about this. When I arrived this morning, I expected this to be an ordinary child welfare investigation. Nothing in Lettie's life was ever ordinary, was it?" Diane did the kindest thing then. She reached out and squeezed my hand as she spoke to me.

"Mostly, her life was extraordinary and in a good way—especially the part of it she shared with you. I have her word for that!" Then Diane spoke to us all.

"Finding out that Lydia Wainwright is dead, and was

murdered by a serial killer, is a huge shock."

"You may find this hard to believe, Diane, but we're all shaken by this too." It's funny how a simple gesture of kindness appears to change the dynamic in a situation. Dahlia morphed into the thoughtful, caring human being she can be at times. "My nephew was in her class with Billie last year. He and his sister will be devastated to learn that she's dead."

"I don't envy you trying to keep all this from becoming a public spectacle that disrupts your ability to find a killer. There's already plenty of scuttlebutt about Ms. Wainwright's failure to report for duty. Most of it is rather nasty—even coming from her family. Good luck keeping a lid on this for long."

"I'm glad you understand what we're up against," Rikki said. "We'd like to apprehend our suspect before word leaks to the community that there's a serial killer on the loose. If we're all on the same page, let's see if Billie has any more bombshells to drop before we move on. We still have to interview Lily and Jesse."

"Where is Billie?" Dahlia asked. That was a good question. I jumped from my seat and ran to look for him. Austin was right behind me.

10

Boy Crazy

WHEN I OPENED the door, I almost tripped over Billie. For a split second, I worried he was dead. Crazy, I know, but murder in real life is still new to me. At the stage we're at now, I'm in hyper-paranoid mode. I dropped to my knees.

"Billie, sweetie, are you okay?" He sat up, bleary-eyed.

"I guess I fell asleep. I do that sometimes." I could understand that if he was roaming around in the woods most of the night instead of sleeping.

"What were you doing out here?"

"I was waiting for someone to invite me in. There's no chair in the hall like outside the principal's office or at Children's Services. So, I sat on the floor. It's more comfortable than I thought it would be. You need to add some splinters or something." He grinned at me, and I could see those dimples.

"Come on in. They're almost done with you—then they'll be grilling me."

"Really, what did you do?" Then his eyes widened. "They don't think you had anything to do with killing Ms.

Wainwright, do they?" My heart sank.

"What else did you hear?" I asked as we walked into the dining room and sat down.

"Nothing. Honest. I guessed about Ms. Wainwright by the way everyone sucked in air when I said her name. We all know she's absent. I almost got into a fight with a kid who said she ran off with someone's husband. I told him that couldn't be true, and to take it back. Before I could punch him, this big girl with lots of long braids, stepped in between us. She told him to shut up because Ms. Wainwright was one of the best teachers she ever had, and her boyfriend isn't married. Then she said the only reason she'd ever ditch school was if she was dead."

"You must mean Brandy Lewis, the ninth-grader."

"Yes, Ms. Constantine."

"What happened then?" I asked.

"Keith said 'sorry.' I couldn't tell if he meant it, or if he was afraid Brandy would get him into trouble with the principal for saying bad things about a teacher. A few of her friends were standing around and heard him say it too. I guess it doesn't matter what he said, does it?" Billie appeared as if he was really upset. "Did the Numbers Man kill Ms. Wainwright? Is it my fault because I told her someone should check on him?"

"Of course not, Billie!" I turned his face toward me and made direct eye contact with him. "What happened to Ms. Wainwright has nothing to do with you. I'll tell you a secret I learned recently. When we lose a person we care about, some of us come up with reasons that it's our fault. That way, we can make believe that we can keep bad things from happening by changing the way we act. What other people do, is about them and not you. That's true about the person who killed Ms. Wainwright and about adults who do terrible things to their kids." Several big, fat tears rolled down Billie's face. My heart went out to him given all he was facing. Not to mention, all that he'd already gone through.

"What's going on in here?" Zelda asked as she burst into the room wearing a black mask and a cowboy hat. "You made him cry, didn't you?" Then she whipped out a bright pink water pistol and squirted Dahlia in the face. Rikki laughed until Melody bounded into the room, dressed in the same getup, and squirted her. The surprised look on Rikki's face was priceless. Billie had a twinkle in his eyes even though his face was still red and splotchy.

"Come on, Billie, your posse has arrived. Ma Tucker sent us to break you out," Zelda added.

"That's Judy, to you," I told Billie.

"Do we need to tie them all up?" Julie asked as she and Carrie stepped into the room with lassos. They were both having trouble delivering their lines without laughing.

"Don't make us haul you off to jail or we'll be forced to dress you in prison orange." Carrie whipped out big orange trash bags like I'd worn last night. "Do you want us to share pictures like these with your colleagues?"

"Oh, no!" I said as they threw wanted posters on the table with me in Slimy Chic. "That's more horrible than I ever dreamed." Maybe it was the belligerent expression on my face or the disgusted look on Hazmat Man's face before he'd donned his mask, but the posters were awful.

"At least you don't stink. Woo-wee, that was rough!"

Austin added grinning. I swatted at him and he ducked.

"Let him have it!" I said, and they nailed him with the squirt guns.

Jesse strode into the room and did a double-take. He acted as if he was in the wrong place, stepped out of the room, and checked both ways before returning. Totally deadpan, he commented.

"I take it the proceedings are in recess." That set off another round of laughs.

"Okay, that was witty, but it's time for the law to take charge," Rikki announced. "I'm ordering you to clear out before Jim calls a paddy wagon to take you all to the…uh. I don't know, somewhere that's not here." Jesse turned to leave.

"Not you, funny man," Dahlia quipped. "Sit!"

Billie was the first one out the door, giving Zelda a high five up high and down low. I was mopping up the water on the table as Diane gathered her belongings.

"I repeat, nothing's ever ordinary around here," Diane said. "I assume I'm free to go?"

"Yes, thanks for all your help," Dahlia said. "I'd like someone to interview Brandy Lewis. Would you be willing to arrange it and sit in on it with her? If she knows who Lydia Wainwright's boyfriend was, that could be important."

"When would you like to interview her?"

"The sooner, the better, Diane," Rikki added as she stopped reorganizing the files in front of her. "You nailed it when you said we're not going to be able to keep any of this from going public for long. The more information we can get before that happens, the less chance we have that people will confuse what they know with what they think they know because it was on television or in social media. Later today or the first thing tomorrow would be best."

"What do I tell Brandy and her parents?" Diane asked.

"Tell them we're interested in speaking with Ms. Wainwright's students given the sudden change in their teacher's behavior," Rikki said.

"If you want to use the reading room to make your calls, make yourself comfortable. If you call Judge Brinkley while you're still here, I can answer any questions he might have. Or if you need to, you can put him on the phone with Rikki or Dahlia," I added.

"Okay, that makes sense," Diane agreed.

"They're welcome to come here for the interview if you can explain why the police want to question Brandy at the Calla Lily Vineyards."

"They might not care where we meet," Diane responded. "Brandy was such a big fan of Lydia, I'm sure she'll be happy to help. Here's an idea. Brandy also has an interest in drama, so if I can offer her a tour of the theater in exchange for being willing to meet on such short notice, that might make all of this more bearable for her."

"That would be fine," I said as I had her follow me to the reading room. I gave her a fax number for Judge Brinkley to use. "The bathroom is that way, and you know where the kitchen is. Help yourself to pop or milk and cookies. Whatever you need to make this work for you. If you have a question, you know where I'll be for the next half hour or so." When I closed the door, I turned around to find Austin standing there.

"Lily, Rikki wants me to get going. She might bring it

up, but if not, I don't want you to worry. I'm visiting a prison inmate who claimed he had information about Penney Lincoln's disappearance years ago. Nothing much came of his testimony because he asked to use it to make a deal on charges he was facing. Nor was anyone very impressed that he'd seen a homeless man speaking to Penney. It may not amount to much, but maybe he got a look at the guy's face or caught a name."

"Why you? Can't someone at the prison ask him?"

"I picked him up as a fugitive a few years ago when he wandered away from a work detail. We made a connection. Rikki's hopeful that he'll talk to me and if he tries to snow me with a bunch of bull, I'll know it."

"Okay. I get it. Why don't you take a box of cookies with you?" I asked.

"I sure will! I've got a long drive ahead of me, so they'll come in handy."

"Nice try, Marshal, but they're not for you. I was hoping you could use the cookies to put your prison pal in a more cooperative mood."

"Do you want to get me locked up for bribery?" he asked, pulling me close.

"Where did she go?" That was Dahlia's voice. She'd be after me any second now. I grabbed Austin's hand, pulled him behind me into the kitchen and, opened the pantry. We only had a few boxes left. Oh, what the heck! Judy and I were going to have to start over baking for the Thanksgiving Harvest Festival organizers.

"Here, take these. One for you and one for the ex-fugitive. Drive safely, save some cookies for the hardened criminal, and get back here as soon as you can."

"Yes, ma'am," he said and kissed me. Then he touched the ring on my finger. "It's a promise."

"I thought I heard your voice," Dahlia said. When I shut the pantry door, she spotted Austin.

"What are you doing in here? You're supposed to be on your way to prison." She smirked at her comment.

"I was arming him with a secret weapon." I held up the boxes of cookies.

"Yeah, right. Let's get this done, so Jesse can get back to tending the fields or whatever else he does around here."

I gave Austin's hand a squeeze as he took the boxes of cookies from me. Then, I swept past Dahlia, slipped into the dining room, and sat in a chair next to Jesse.

"What do you want to know?" I asked before Dahlia could take her seat. Jim Brady had left, so only the two women remained.

"Austin told us you were both acquainted with Penney Lincoln, and you have information about her that runs counter to her mother's statement that she didn't have a boyfriend."

"When you put it like that, maybe she wasn't trying to mislead anyone. From what I heard, she didn't have 'a' boyfriend; she had lots of them. I was new to the area, so I didn't know Penney well. She was in the same class as me in middle school—cute, funny, but not a good student. She didn't seem too interested in being a good student, and she was in trouble from the day school started. Then one day, not long after school had started, I heard she was gone."

"I'm going to tell you the same thing," Jesse said. "Because I was a couple of years older than Penney, I didn't know her personally. I recognized her when I saw her, and most of what I can tell you is from gossip. There was plenty of it once she disappeared, but even before that, I heard more than one person call her 'boy crazy.'"

"Maybe no one wanted to challenge her grieving mother," I murmured. "That's too bad because if they had, someone might have figured out that she wasn't ever coming home because one of her boyfriends had killed her."

"Maybe not, Lily. If the police had asked me, I would have told them she ran away with some guy. That wouldn't have helped find her either. In fact, it's almost too easy to use that as a reason not to carry out a more thorough investigation."

"Jesse's made a good point. 'Possible runaway,' is noted in her record. The investigators don't mention a boyfriend, but her mother told them she'd run away before."

"Running away with a boyfriend would make more sense if she was sixteen or seventeen, but she was Billie's age—twelve or thirteen, right?" I asked.

"Kids even younger than Billie runaway, but most of them are older. In Penney Lincoln's case, she was a few days shy of fifteen. That she was a poor student is an understatement. She failed the second and sixth grades, so she was closer in age to you, Jesse, than to Lily."

"Okay, well I saw her hanging out after school with boys my age. I don't remember a specific one, but I guess she didn't mind if they were younger than her."

"Or older," Jesse added. "More than one person told me she was going out with a 'college boy.' I assume that meant a man in his twenties."

"Did you ever see her with an older guy?" I asked.

"I saw her get into a car with a male at the wheel. I didn't see him, but he had an expensive, nice-looking car. A black Camaro that was in great condition—almost as if it had just been driven off the lot. I doubt it belonged to some high schooler."

"Thanks, Jesse," Rikki said. "Was he on the school grounds at the time?"

"No. He was waiting for Penney on the street in front of the school."

"That's too bad. I was hoping he was someone known to the administration."

"Maybe a teacher or someone in charge noticed. I wasn't the only one ogling the car. He got plenty of attention, especially when he burned rubber driving away. Good luck finding someone who's still around twenty years later and remembers an incident like that. I was a kid who envied the guys who could afford cars." Jesse shrugged.

"When Penney's mother told the police she'd run away before, did she give them a reason? Had she reported her disappearance to the police?" I asked, just wondering out loud since it was none of my business.

"We've only had a short time to review the old case," Dahlia said. "So far, I don't see a previous missing persons report. There's something vague in her mother's statement about Penney not being happy about the rules at home."

"If you prepare her for another shock, you could enlist Diane to review the Children's Services records, if they go back that far," I suggested. "Even if they don't, she might know someone who was around then who was familiar with the family and any problems they had with Penney. You've already contacted Judge Brinkley. Didn't he confirm what we've said about Penney's boyfriend problems?"

"I'm not sure what he can tell us since he was representing Penney's mother and stepfather at the time. Contacting him was a courtesy call because his name is in the record and I didn't want him to be surprised by a nosy reporter. What makes you so sure he knew about her *boyfriend problems?*" Dahlia used her fingers to make those little quote marks as she repeated my words.

"I, um, I'm not sure why I said that," I stuttered. "Now that I think about it, I could have mixed up what he said with something reported in the media. I'm sure I saw him on television with Penney's parents. When Penney first disappeared, Rachel Lincoln was on the air begging for information about her daughter." Dahlia peered at me trying to gauge my truthfulness. If she planned on interrogating me further, Jesse put a stop to it.

"Yeah, well Mrs. Lincoln wasn't always so great on camera. She was hysterical at times and chewed out the police about not doing more. Don't say I'm being too hard on a desperate parent because she was like that before Penney vanished. I remember a visit she made to elementary school. She was angry that Penney was in detention and threw a huge fit. I was waiting for her to punch the vice principal. No wonder she hired an attorney, she had to be a prime suspect."

"All parents are suspects when a child goes missing, but maybe they had more reason to be worried than most," Rikki murmured.

"Penney must have been embarrassed. I would have been humiliated, Jesse."

"She was. Maybe that's another reason it was so easy for me to believe she'd finally found some guy who could get her out of there."

"Okay, so that makes me even more certain Children's Services is the way to go," I argued. "Diane's already mixed up in all of this, so you won't have to call on anyone else to dig into Penney Lincoln's family background. Diane must qualify for extra duty pay. I hope she's got a good therapist."

"Anyone who does the work she does, day after day, has to learn how to deal with compassion fatigue and secondhand trauma," Rikki sighed. "We're pushing the limits, though, I'm sure."

"At least she's not sleep-deprived, like you two are." Rikki and Dahlia both nodded. "Do you want me to speak to Diane about Penney Lincoln?"

"No, we should try to restore some sort of boundaries between us, the professionals who assist us, and our witnesses," Rikki said smiling. "I'll tell her what we'd like her to do for us now. Once we know when the Lewis family is planning to visit, I'm heading to my hotel for a nap."

"You don't need to do that. We have plenty of places for you to sleep. When Ma Tucker returns with her gang, we'll fix lunch, and you can join us. You too, Dahlia."

"Thanks, Lily. A chair in a quiet corner will do it for me." That's when all our phones began to ring.

11

Dustin's Debut

I RAN THROUGH the butler's pantry and grabbed the phone in the kitchen. I heard Jesse shout, "Where?" Then he ran past me and out the backdoor.

"Lily?"

"Yes? What is it, Judy?"

"He's here. The Numbers Man." Judy spoke in hushed tones.

"Where?"

"In the basement of the theater building."

"Jesse's on his way." I heard the front door slam as I said that. That had to be Dahlia or Rikki or maybe both women. "Rikki and Dahlia too. Let me go get them and tell them where you are."

"No, no, please don't do that. Is there any way you can get over here without attracting attention? The guy says he needs to talk to you and that it's very important."

"Why me?"

"He hasn't told us. Will you just get over here? Billie says to tell you please not to bring the police or say a word to them. He doesn't want anyone to get hurt."

"Okay. I don't want him to hurt Billie," I cried. A gasp from behind me caused my heart to jump into my throat. I'd forgotten all about poor Diane. Spotting her gave me an idea though.

"Judy wants me to go to the theater building. She says the man we've been looking for is in the basement and he's got Billie. Billie's asked me not to say a word to the police. Will you come with me? If we get stopped, you can say I'm showing you the way to the theater building so you can check on Billie or bring him back to the house or something like that. For some reason, the Numbers Man wants to speak to me."

"We could stand here and argue about it, but let's go. I won't lie for you, though. Billie didn't tell me not to speak to the police." Before she could utter another word or change her mind, I ran for the front door. Diane shut the door and followed me down the steps from the porch, taking a little longer to navigate them in the pumps she wore.

I made a beeline for the theater, taking the shortest route to the cover of the trees Aunt Lettie had planted around the theater grounds. I could hear shouts off in the distance and saw Dahlia's police car careening down the main road to the entrance gate. I hoped they were moving too fast to have seen us.

Once we were hidden by the trees, I ran down the middle aisle to the stage. When I turned to mount the steps to the stage, Diane was only a few steps behind me. She'd kicked off her pumps and was carrying them as she ran in her bare feet.

"Thank goodness I didn't skip my water aerobics class this week!"

She was breathing hard, and so was I. "This had better not be another prank, or I'll call Judge Brinkley and ask him to rescind his order placing Billie in your care. Now what?"

"Up the stairs to the stage and then down the backstage stairs to the basement. After that, we improvise." Minutes later, we were at the door leading into the huge lower level. When I turned the knob the door was locked, so I knocked.

"Who is it?"

"Billie, is that you?"

"Yes! I knew you'd come." He opened the door wide and then closed it a little. "Ms. Constantine, you're still here."

"Yes I am. I have good news for you from Judge Brinkley." She spoke in a chirpy voice, but there was anxiety written all over her face.

"Stay here while I see if I can fix this, okay?"

Fix what? I wondered as Billie shut the door.

"How odd," I muttered.

"You're surprised by odd?" We both shut up when Billie opened the door and told us to come in. As soon as we were inside, he shut the door and locked it. A man stood in the shadows near the cement walls beneath the windows. He was shielded from the sunlight that streamed in through the half-windows placed above us at ground level.

Judy and my diva friends were sitting around a large worktable piled high with all sorts of tools and supplies. I don't believe I'd ever seen all of them so quiet at once. When Marlowe saw me, he began to whine and wiggle.

He squirmed away from Carrie, ran, and sprang into my arms. Dustin stepped backward.

"It's okay, Dustin. See how much the little dog trusts her? Lily won't hurt you and she won't let anyone else hurt you either." Billie sounded too mature for a twelve-year-old.

A breeze blew in from an open window and an unpleasant odor came from where the Numbers Man stood. Nothing as foul-smelling as the slime pit. More horsey—like old, dirty hay. His hair and clothes were dirty. There was mud caked on his boots.

"These ladies are helping me. They can help you if you let them." Billie took Dustin's hand and brought him closer to us. Dustin's head was down. "This is Lily."

"I know who she is. I saw her when she was small with a happy face. She wore hats and clothes and talked in different voices. I liked to watch her run through the woods with the other girls." It took me a moment to process what he'd said. Not only that he'd been watching us, but he'd been living in the woods for twenty years. How was that possible?

"Dustin, if you were watching us, why didn't you join us?" I asked.

"I was too big and wrinkled like an old man. I didn't want to scare you. After they took Billie off the fence, I heard him. It made me sad that I scared him even when he couldn't see me. He was good at watching me in the woods and I made sure the Sitter never hurt him."

"Dustin says he didn't hurt Ms. Wainwright, but that it was his fault—until I told him what you said, Lily. That what other people do is about them, not us. Dustin never hurt anyone—the Sitter did it."

"Is that true, Dustin?" I asked.

"Yes. It was my job to watch over the bodies, so they didn't get out. I did something wrong, they're out, and now the Sitter's got to fix it. I came to tell Billie I'm sorry I scared him and I'm sorry the bodies got out."

"Judy told you that's not your fault either. Coyotes and the rain did it," Billie reminded Dustin.

"If you didn't hurt anyone, and the Sitter did, why don't you want us to call the police?" I asked.

"Because they'll blame me like they did when the house burned down."

"Show Lily your arm." Billie lifted Dustin's hand and slid up one of his jacket sleeves. It didn't move much, but it was easy to see scarring.

"I'm so sorry. Did the Sitter set the house on fire?" I asked.

"No. He told me my sister's body got out. She set the house on fire to kill Mom and Dad. When I told the police, they said I was lying and took me to a place where there weren't any woods."

"That must have made you very unhappy," I said. "How did you get back here to the woods?"

"Go on, you can tell Lily," Billie urged.

Then one of the women at the table sneezed. Dustin bolted. In a split second, he was on top of the boxes stacked next to the windows. When he raised his head to steady himself, even in the shadows I could see that his face was badly burned. I also knew he wasn't the man who had glared at me from the fiery darkness during the savage storm.

"Come down, please, Dustin. I have so many questions for you. My friends will make room for us at the table, and you can tell me more. Billie says you know lots about numbers. I'd like you to teach me about the numbers, okay?"

"That's not what I wanted to tell you. Watch out for the Sitter. Don't be fooled because his face is bright and shiny. His heart is dark. He's even better than you were at pretending, and he says it's your fault, Lily."

"Dustin, I'm scared. What's my fault? Come down here, please, and tell me who he is." He appeared to be considering it when there was a ruckus outside the basement door Billie had opened for Diane and me. Then there was banging on the door at the opposite end of the room. Distracted by the noise I turned away, and when I turned back around, Dustin was gone. The window clattered shut.

"Judy, will you answer that door while I get this one?" When I opened the door, Dahlia was standing there with her gun drawn. Before I could speak, she brushed past me doing that thing I'd seen cops do during filming. Pointing the gun one way and then another, Dahlia scanned the room until she reached Jesse, who'd come in the other way. Rikki stood next to Jesse.

"What are you all doing now?" Dahlia asked, putting her gun in its holster. "Why do you stink like an old barn?"

"It's not me. You just scared off the Numbers Man. If you'd given us a few more minutes, we could probably have turned him over to you so you could take him into protective custody." It took Dahlia only about thirty seconds to figure out the only other way out of the room was through the windows.

"Go, you guys!" Dahlia ordered. "Search every inch of the property between here and the woods. He can't sneak around during the day like he does at night."

I didn't challenge her as two uniformed officers ran out the door and up the steps. Still, Dustin had managed to get onto the property in broad daylight. Jesse's security patrol and the police patrols hadn't seen him. I remembered what Austin had said earlier about the Numbers Man being so much more familiar with the property than the rest of us.

"If you'd read us in on what you planned to do, we might have been able to help. Jesse got a phone call about the Numbers Man and one of the officers who took Jim's place called Dahlia. One of the vineyard pickers flagged us down and said he saw someone go into the theater from the stage. Am I right to assume that the call you took was from one of these folks?" Rikki eyed the women sitting around the table.

"Don't blame Lily or anyone else. I'm the one who told her to get over here as fast as she could without talking to the police. I may have led her to believe that Billie was in danger when he wasn't," Judy said.

"If Lily believed Billie was in danger, that was more reason to involve us, not less," Rikki said, shaking her head as if she'd had it. I'd say Rikki was doing a little counting now—to ten maybe as she struggled to regain her composure. "Start at the beginning and explain what happened. Then you're all going home and you're not setting foot outside without express permission from Dahlia or me."

"Excuse me!" Zelda said, jumping out of her seat. She was winding up to chew Rikki out.

"Are we under arrest?" Melody asked as she reached over and tugged on Zelda's sleeve.

"Not yet. For now, I'm putting you all into protective custody for your own good, and my sanity. Say another word, though, and Dahlia will start making arrests." Melody yanked Zelda's arm hard and made her sit. "Now give us the scoop about the Numbers Man. I take it he came in through the window since that's the way he left."

"Yes, we'd left a window open to get rid of the musty smell," Judy explained. "Billie came down here to get some scissors and straight pins for us. When he didn't come back quickly, I was worried that he was having trouble finding the sewing supplies. I stepped through the door, and the Numbers Man dragged Billie into the shadows."

"We were talking, and when Judy came in, he got scared. I told Judy that his name was Dustin, and he wasn't going to hurt me. He came out in the daytime to tell us he'd never hurt anyone because he knows what pain feels like."

"I'm sorry we've ticked you off, Rikki. I don't believe the Numbers Man is the killer, but he knows who it is. I'm as upset as you are that he disappeared again. It's not like I had time to call and check things out with you." I avoided Dahlia's gaze, afraid of what she might say if I looked at her the wrong way. "If I'd told you the troubled man you believe killed five people was in here, would you have waited to hear him out before scaring him so badly that he became catatonic?"

"Probably not, but that wasn't your call to make. This is a serious police investigation, and I'm warning all of you to lie low, or I'm going to turn Dahlia loose. Now someone please fill us in on Dustin, the Numbers Man's, theatrical debut."

Judy and Billie were able to do that in less than five minutes. His visit had been a short one. He'd repeated himself a lot when I got here, so I'd heard most of what he'd had to say.

"How much of what he's says can we believe?" Diane asked me.

"He's obviously very confused, but he's not lying. I believe him when he says he didn't hurt anyone. Whether he understands it or not, though, he's shielded a killer for years. The scars are real, so he was in a fire. I can also tell you that there was a second man in the woods during the storm. I saw him, and he fits the bill as the angry man Dustin calls the Sitter."

"Yeah, that guy had two mean eyes. This poor guy only has one good eye, and he's not mean—except to himself." Julie's comment was tinged with sadness.

"I was wrong about him being an old man, wasn't I?" Billie asked. "He sounded almost like a regular guy today."

"You heard him. He considers himself old because his face is wrinkled—from the scars. That could be why he speaks like an old man sometimes. It's hard to say how old he is, Billie. Did he give you his last name or say when or where his parents' house burned down?"

"No, Lily. It happened a long time ago is all he said—before I was born."

"From what he said about watching you and your friends play in the woods, he already had those scars then. With burns like his, he must have been hospitalized. Even if he was initially cared for in a burn unit when he was transferred into custodial care, he would have needed rehab," Diane sounded glum about Dustin's situation. "Rikki, Dahlia, I understand you need to find Dustin, but you won't shoot him, will you? There's a childlike quality about him. I'd say he's a middle-aged man, but he seemed to relate better to Billie than to the adult in the room."

"We'll do our best to apprehend him with as little force as possible. It doesn't sound like he was armed," Dahlia commented. Everyone in the room shook their heads, or whispered, "no." "No matter what we do, he's going to be scared. By the way he talks about the Sitter, he's already scared, and has been for a long time. We'll be doing Dustin a favor to pick him up."

I had to admit Dahlia was probably right. When I'd come running to the theater without screaming for help from the police, I'd imagined the Numbers Man holding Billie hostage at knifepoint. Now, all I could think about was what poor Dustin had yet to face with the man he called the Sitter. Questions whirled in my head at a dizzying pace.

"You know what? I'm ready to head home and let these folks do their jobs. Did you arrange for Brandy and her parents to visit us this afternoon, Diane?"

"No, but they've agreed to come out here early tomorrow morning if the entire place isn't on lockdown. Brandy's very excited to meet you, Lily, and hear what it's like to be an actress. She's also looking forward to touring the theater."

"That was probably another error in judgment on our part, but since it's set, let's go with it," Rikki said. I guess she assumed I wouldn't object to the idea, but she and Dahlia hadn't bothered to ask. What else was I going to do now that I'd been grounded?

"It's fine with me. I'm happy to speak with her, Diane."

"Have you all cleared out or do you need to get back into the Calla Lily Detention Center to collect vital police documents lying on my dining room table before you bar the doors and windows?" I didn't wait for a reply. I grabbed Billie's hand and left the basement practically flying up the stairs.

"Are you angry or scared?" Billie asked.

"Both. How about you?" I asked.

"Both, but I'm mostly worried about Dustin. I wish I knew where he lived, so I could talk him into staying in the Calla Lily Detention Center with us. He needs to tell us who the Sitter is, except that Dustin says he's not sure."

"What does that mean?" I asked, stopping for an instant as we reached the edge of the trees surrounding the theater.

"When he and his sister were little, they called him one name, and then when he took Dustin out of the place with no woods, he told him a different name, and when he got back here, he had another one. That's why he just calls him the Sitter." I heard voices behind us, and I really wasn't ready to be cordial to Rikki and Dahlia quite yet.

"Let's go, Billie. I understand how you feel, but you're not going to go look for him. Dustin knows how to deal with the Sitter much better than we do." Billie nodded.

"Okay."

"Promise?" I asked, and pointed to the ring on my finger.

"Yes," he replied and crossed his heart.

"I'll race you to the deck," I said taking off, so he had to hustle catch up with me. My lead vanished in no time, but Marlowe beat us both.

12

Countdown to Murder

WHEN I REACHED for the doorknob, it turned at once. I wished that I'd locked it before fleeing. I opened the door cautiously. "Maybe we should wait for the rest to catch up with us," I muttered.

"Why? If there's anyone inside who shouldn't be in there, Marlowe will tell us, won't he?"

"Yes. You're so smart, aren't you?" I asked as I opened the door a little more and Marlowe dashed into the kitchen.

"Mostly, I'm just in a hurry to get to the restroom. Excuse me," Billie said and ran for it.

My brain was still overflowing with a jumble of questions. Was the Sitter the one who'd conjured up the story about needing to sit beside the graves to keep the bodies from rising from the grave? Had he set the fire that destroyed to Dustin's home and killed his parents? How had Dustin's sister died, and why was she buried in the woods? How was any of what's happened my fault?

I peeked into the dining room. Dahlia and Rikki had left things behind. I got a box to load their items. At

Dahlia's seat, a folder was open, and I glimpsed a printed copy of an email from Ben. I scanned it quickly, trying to commit the information to memory while puzzling about it. Then, I sucked in a big breath when I read the last item.

When my phone rang, I darted into the kitchen, leaving the box on the dining room table. I grabbed my cellphone from the kitchen counter as the room exploded into a riot of noise and activity. As my friends burst into the room, all talking at once, Darjeeling took off after Marlowe, yipping happily. She ran in circles around Billie's feet until he picked her up.

"Hello," I said amid the raucous outburst.

"Lily, is everything all right? I got cc'd on a text from Rikki that we now have an updated description and a first name for an intruder at the Calla Lily Vineyards after he broke into the theater building. He's wanted for questioning about a series of murders that occurred in the area over several decades. Is Billie, okay?"

"It's good to hear no one's issued a 'shoot to kill order,'" I groused. "Austin, we're all fine," I said loud enough for Judy to hear me.

I left the kitchen, hoping to find a quieter spot and the doorbell rang. That had to be Rikki and Dahlia coming to pick up their files since they weren't in the kitchen with everyone else.

"I'll get it!" I shouted and ran to the door. Much to my surprise, it was an old family friend. "One more minute, Austin, please."

"Dr. Kennedy, how are you?" I said, hugging the man who'd been my physician for a decade before I moved to LA.

"I'm as good as a man can be who's pushing eighty. Judy said you need me to examine a boy who's staying with you and injured himself on your fence. Are you doing okay?"

"If you're asking about losing Aunt Lettie, I miss her every day. Judy keeps telling me she's still with us—in every inch of this house."

"Judy's a wise woman." As Dr. Kennedy uttered her name, she magically appeared.

"Doctor K, you're a lifesaver," Judy said as she bustled down the hall.

"If it's that serious, you ought to call an ambulance," he said giving me a little wink. "I'm here to give the rascal a tetanus shot, and maybe a lecture about not climbing other people's fences."

"That's exactly what he needs," Judy replied. "Let's go meet him." As they were about to leave, the doorbell rang again. That was my cue to run for it. I dashed through the parlor and into a room set up with comfy chairs and a large flat screen television hanging on the wall. It was a stretch to call it a media room.

"Sorry. That's our old family doctor—making a house call, if you can believe it. Judy must have come up with the idea since Rikki and Dahlia have placed us under house arrest."

"Uh, oh. How did you manage that?" he asked in a light-hearted way.

"Didn't Rikki call and bring you up to speed? They got that new info because we had a daytime encounter with Dustin, the Numbers Man. Granted, the additional information he gave us about his background isn't much.

It might give you a few more questions to ask if there's a lull in the conversation with your *'pen pal.'*"

"I've got a meeting with him at the penitentiary first thing in the morning. I'll tell him you called him that and see what he has to say."

"Make sure you give him my address. That way, when he gets out, he can come looking for me. He'll have to get in line behind the Sitter."

"The what?"

"I can explain, although Rikki will give you a different point of view on the entire incident." I did my best to be straight with Austin. As I retold the story, it seemed more stupid than it had at the time. I was almost ready to apologize for my behavior when Austin reacted.

"I can't leave you alone for a day, can I?" His voice was filled with worry.

"Under the circumstances, I'm not sure what else I could have done. I ran in almost a blind panic when Judy called."

"I might have gone along with your idea, but I would have asked Jesse to post his guys around the building to grab Dustin if he fled." Austin sighed.

"Jesse might have done that if I'd asked. I honestly didn't think of it as an option. You've had to deal with fugitives climbing out of windows to escape—this is all new to me."

"True. Please, don't take any more chances. The information Dustin gave you may come in handy when I have my meeting tomorrow. I didn't read any reference to the fact that the homeless guy he saw speaking to Penney Lincoln was badly burned. That could have been enough to get the police to discount the guy as a love interest or a threat to their missing teen if he had told them." Then he paused. I already knew what he was going to say because I'd said something like it to myself. "No amount of information is worth risking an encounter with the Sitter, or whatever his real name may be."

"I understand. Did you also get cc'd on the email from Hazmat Man?"

"How did you find about that?" Austin was on the verge of becoming exasperated.

"Purely by accident, promise! I'm not sure why this popped into my mind, but when I was reading the email it dawned on me that Ms. Wainwright disappeared at the same time of the year as Penney Lincoln."

"Yes, that wasn't in the email. Did you or a member of your diva posse get that from Ben?"

"Good grief, it's not that hard to figure out. Maybe it was the mention in the email that the murders took place a decade apart—except for the woman who burned to death and was buried with her child. From what Dustin told us about the fire, that must be his mother and his sister. I wonder if all the numbers Billie found in the woods have something to do with the death of his sister or his mother, and that's why Dustin wore the black armband."

"If you're talking about an anniversary date, it's odd that the murders didn't occur more often. From what Dustin told you, with his roundabout, magical thinking about his sister returning from the grave, Dustin's made a connection between her death and the most recent murder."

"It's not the first time he made that connection, either.

Dustin also said his sister came back from her grave and set fire to the house, killing his parents. Maybe the murders are timed to coincide with a specific way in which the numbers line up, and it doesn't happen often, so the murders are far apart."

"Billie believed Dustin was counting down to an event last night—maybe it was a countdown to murder."

"Two murders," I mumbled. "Will they charge the killer for the murder of Lydia Wainwright's unborn child?"

"I assume so. You didn't miss a thing, did you? I'm sorry you got your hands on that email message."

"I would have heard about it one way or another. No way can you keep news like that from leaking to the press. Six murders! You've got to stop this guy."

"We're working on it. Rikki has people digging into old news about fires in which there were fatalities thirty or forty years ago. And about children that died or went missing not long before that. That's in addition to searching police records for information about women in their twenties who disappeared between 1999 and 2019 since the identity of the victim killed around 2009 hasn't been determined. Maybe there's a more specific date in Billie's notebook that can help. Did anyone go to his house and get it?"

"Not yet. After lunch, Diane's going to retrieve it, along with Billie's schoolbooks and clothes. At least he'll have something to wear besides Angels' baseball gear since I can't take him shopping now that I'm grounded."

"It takes more to tick off Rikki than Dahlia, but her judgment is swift and final. Don't put up a fight or you'll dig your way into a deeper hole." I harrumphed.

"She can't expect me to play hostess, can she? I'm not making her more coffee and cookies, and she can take a nap in the backseat of her car. The B&B is closed to uninvited guests and I'm rolling up the welcome mat until she sets us free. That's not true for Diane, who's still here. We'll welcome Brandy and her family members who are going to be allowed through the gates in the morning."

"What about me?" Austin asked.

"You're the best lawman I've ever met, so you're still welcome to visit. Hopefully, once we get out of this mess, the only dead bodies will be in the movies we watch. On second thought, maybe not even in the movies. I'd really like you to have a chance for you to enjoy the vineyards and experience them the way I did growing up."

"We've had evenings like that—watching the sunset from the porch. Now that Billie says you're my girl, I'll sit a little closer."

"Promise?"

"Yes, and I also promise to try to get back in time for dinner tomorrow night. I'll be your armed escort so I can spring you for a dinner out on the town."

"Good luck, Cowboy. I doubt even your most disarming smile can get Marshal Rikki to issue a reprieve until this case is closed."

"You could be right. I'd enjoy dinner more if you didn't need an armed escort. Speaking of food, I need to figure out where to get some chow around here."

I should have hung up when he said that, but I wasn't ready to let him go. I missed him. I'd found a quiet, comfortable hiding place, free from the intrusion of doorbells, snarky detectives, and crime scenes. Who knew when that would happen again? I kept him talking a few more minutes. Selfish, I know, but even Austin's small talk makes me laugh. Then the conversation took a more serious turn.

"I know you're not happy about being confined to the house, but it's a relief since I can't be there for another day or so."

"I don't like the idea that the Sitter believes something that's going on is my fault. Come home soon, Marshal."

"As soon as I can. I'll see you tomorrow night, Calla Lily."

When I stepped out into the parlor, the most amazing aroma reached me. I almost ran to the kitchen.

"What is that wonderful smell?" I asked. I couldn't believe my eyes when I saw Doctor Kennedy wearing an apron tied at the waist, standing at the stove cooking. "Who put you to work?"

"The doctor says I'm super healthy so my checkup went fast, although he says I should probably lay off the chicken fried steak a little. I told him that's not a problem because I never ate it before."

"Can you believe that?" Vernon asked. I wasn't sure what to say in response to the doctor since it's hardly regarded as a healthy dish these days. "He's never had mashed potatoes made from freshly boiled potatoes, either, or succotash." Then he pointed at Zelda.

"When your sassy Latina friend said she hasn't had chicken fried steak either, I had Jim Brady make an emergency run to the butcher shop to pick up a dozen well-pounded cube steaks."

"He did that?" I asked. "And Dahlia let him?" You could have pushed me over with a feather.

"Why wouldn't he? If it weren't for me, he wouldn't still be with us. When he first joined the force, he got a nasty bite wresting a broken bottle from a mean drunk. Instead of going to the ER as he was advised to do, he tried to care for the wound himself. By the time he came to see me, he was a very sick man, and loopy from fever." Doctor Kennedy staggered around to emphasize his point.

"I'm not sure Jim told Dahlia what he was doing, Lily. He delivered the steaks to the backdoor." Judy's eyes sparkled mischievously. "I told him to come back and we'd have a plate ready for him."

"You can get that ready for him now," Doctor Kennedy announced." The gravy is perfect, even if I do say so myself."

The entire posse went into action in assembly-line fashion. When Jim came to the door to claim his meal, I figured he might as well come inside and eat with us. He'd be at the house soon anyway to walk Diane to her car and then escort her to Billie's family home.

The meal was delicious. My cowboy would have loved it. Folks scattered once lunch was over and we'd cleaned up. Diane left with Jim Brady to claim Billie's things and inspect the living conditions at his home. After the morning we'd had, I was ready for a nap since I was housebound, but Judy had something else in mind.

13

A Wappo Curse

"THANKS FOR COOKING such a wonderful lunch, Vernon. Before you leave, do you want you to try one of the Calla Lily wines we're entering in the Taste of Napa Challenge?" Judy had already begun opening a chilled bottle of the amazing Chardonnay Aunt Lettie and the winery's chief winemaker had created.

"I'd be delighted. Shall we sit out on the porch? I don't want to distress the boy, but I'd like to get the scoop on why the vineyard has become Fort Calla Lily. Jesse was carrying a rifle when I came in through the gate."

"We'll do our best," I said. "Nothing's very clear right now. The police don't just come right out and brief us, although we keep stumbling into the middle of the investigation. They don't appreciate that much."

I'd already tried the wine, but since it was a new bottle, I went through the routine Aunt Lettie had taught me before I was legally allowed to drink. Of course, wine tasters typically spit out the wine after tasting it. Most of the time, that's what I did at sixteen.

I held up the glass Judy had poured for me and gazed

at its glistening white color, tinged with gold. This vintage was a lighter color because it had spent less time in oak barrels. When I poked my nose into the glass, the aroma was fresh with a bit of the fruit still discernible. A peachy flavor tinged with vanilla lingered as I swallowed the wine after swishing it in my mouth.

"What do you make of it, Vernon?" Judy asked. I still hadn't gotten used to the idea of calling my old family doctor by his first name, even though it made more sense than referring to him as Doctor Kennedy.

"A dry, lively wine with a light fruity flavor, it rolls off the tongue with a hint of butter. Sublime!" He grabbed the open bottle from the kitchen counter and led us down the hallway to the foyer and outside onto the porch. The light had begun to soften in the late afternoon sun, adding a golden glow to everything it touched. The ever-changing play of light and shadow throughout the day is one of my favorite features of life in wine country.

This afternoon, the rain had left everything clean and fresh. I loved the smell of good, clean dirt from the first time I set foot in the vineyards. Until they'd spent a few days here, my diva friends hadn't understood what I meant. It's not just the rain that coaxes the scent from the fertile vineyard soil; when the sun bakes the earth, it gives off a wonderful almost toasty fragrance.

As soon as we were settled into our comfy seats, Judy gave Vernon a brief overview of recent events. I remained silent until she'd finished and then shared what I'd discovered from reading the email from Ben and filled them in on Austin's assignment.

I wanted our visitor to hear everything we'd learned

since I thought I'd guessed Judy's reason for asking Vernon to stick around. The doctor had been delivering babies and caring for residents of the Napa Valley for more than half a century. He'd grown up here and had only been away while he was in college and medical school. Vernon's a living encyclopedia of the area's history.

"Six deaths? This is alarming news. It's going to wreak havoc in the community unless the police can nab the culprit soon." He peered over his glasses at me, and I squirmed in my seat. "It's too bad that young lawman wasn't with you when you had this Dustin fellow corralled in the basement."

"Yes, I know. I almost had Dustin coaxed into telling us more. He's been living with fear and confusion for a long time. Dustin wants to unburden himself, but he's as terrified of the authorities as he is of the man he calls the Sitter."

"I wonder, Vernon, if any of this means more to you than it does to the rest of us. I'm guessing Dustin is at least forty years old. You were still delivering most of the babies back in the late seventies. He had a sister who disappeared or died about a year before both parents were killed in a fire. The boy was burned badly."

"I do remember something about a fire. A child was brought into the emergency room. I didn't know the family well because they were reclusive. They were odd and kept to themselves and there were all sorts of ridiculous rumors about them when I was a kid."

"What kind of rumors?" I asked.

"That the family was into witchcraft and black magic.

Older kids told me not even to look at them if I ran into one of them because I'd turn into a frog or a stone. I don't know how people resolved the belief in how powerful they were with the rumors that they were doomed because of a curse."

"Cursed? Where did that idea come from?" I asked the doctor in amazement. Judy sat up straighter in her chair and leaned in as she spoke.

"You're talking about the Watkins family, aren't you?" she asked Vernon. "I haven't thought about them in years. When I was around ten years old, I never saw them again. That was long before the fire you're talking about. If anyone had asked, I would have said they'd left the valley. I thought the curse was on their land because it was sacred to the Wappo tribe."

"Yes, I heard about the Wappo Curse, too." Vernon responded, staring off into the distance as if that's where the past resided. "That never made sense, either, because most of the indigenous people died or left the area after Mexican Independence. That would have been before we Anglos arrived. Apart from calling the valley 'Napa' like the Wappo did, many of the Wappo tribe members had been killed taking their heritage and history with them"

"Even if they didn't come into town, Judy, they still lived here since that's where Dustin was burned so badly and his parents perished in a fire."

"I never heard a word about it," Judy said. "Forty years ago, you were still working at the old Calistoga Clinic and Hospital. Is that how you found out about it?"

"Yes. We didn't have the facilities to care for the child, so he was rushed to a burn unit in San Francisco. I lost track of him at that point."

"Wasn't there a scandal that the cursed child of a cursed family was blamed for killing his parents?" I asked.

"The boy couldn't have been more than five years old at the time. I never heard anyone say a word about blaming him for the fire. If the man you spoke to is Dustin Watkins, he is confused. Children do blame themselves for such traumatic events." I nodded since Billie and I had discussed that very thing with the Numbers Man.

"Did a family member call the fire department? If his parents were killed in the fire how did he get to the hospital?" Judy asked.

"A neighbor who lived some distance from Watkins' homestead reported the fire. The boy had somehow managed to get out of the house. Maybe that's why he blames himself—survivor guilt. Members of the fire department brought him in. They said the house and most of the barn had burned to the ground. I don't believe it was until the next day that authorities found the bodies of his parents. I don't recall ever hearing that another child lived there, or that the Watkins had any other relatives."

"The crime scene investigators have established that the bodies of a child and her mother were found, together, at the original burial site in the woods. The child's mother was killed in a fire. All the other victims, including the child, died from a blow to the back of the head. It must be Dustin's mother and sister, although I don't understand how they ended up in the woods, or where his father's body is buried. Most of what Dustin says about his sister getting out of her grave and killing his parents by setting the fire doesn't make sense, except the idea that she died before their parents did," I said as I let Judy pour me another glass of wine.

"That must be true. Her body was found last, which means she was buried first. What if Dustin killed his sister and his parents buried her in the woods rather than report her death to the police?" Judy asked. "They might not have been able to stand the thought of losing both children, even if they knew Dustin had killed her. That would be a reason for him to blame himself or to be afraid her body would rise up and seek revenge."

"Maybe," I said skeptically. "What about all the other murders? How was he able to survive for twenty years in the woods without being seen in town by someone? How did he lure new victims into the woods? Besides, Dustin says he's never hurt anyone, and I believe him."

"Well, the forensics evidence ought to be able to determine if a four-year-old child could have inflicted the blow to the back of his sister's head."

"That would help answer one of my questions," I said. "I have so many others. Where did Dustin go after he was taken to the hospital in San Francisco if he had no family? I assume members of the fire department investigated the blaze. Did they find out what caused it? Do they keep records that long? If he's Dustin Watkins, we have a last name. I'll call Diane Constantine, from Children's Services. Digging up old information about a boy named Dustin, burned in a fire forty years ago, ought to be a little easier with his last name. You've been a huge help."

"I'm amazed at how well you're doing after all that's gone on in less than twenty-four hours. You may have the name and mien of a delicate flower, Lily, but you're obviously a steel magnolia like your aunt."

"That's sweet of you to say. I'll need to be strong now that I've promised to look after Billie for a while."

"That lawman will be at your side to help, won't he?" He eyed the ring on my finger as he asked the question. I blushed.

"It's a promise ring," I replied. "At this point, it's a promise to be best friends."

"Then you're off to a good start. Marriages founded on a deep and abiding friendship are loving and sturdy." I wasn't sure how to respond, but I managed to nod in agreement.

"She's a strong-willed steel magnolia. You won't get more out of her. It's only been weeks since they met, not years, or so Lily keeps reminding me."

I didn't say anything to Judy. I'd said weeks, not months when I reminded her about the short time that I'd known Austin. Promising to be friends by wearing his Grandmother's ring was a huge step despite all the good feelings I have about the wonderful man.

"Love runs on a clock that ticks in here," Vernon said, pointing to his heart.

"She'll figure that out. We'll invite you to the wedding, and that's a promise," Judy quipped, squeezing my hand.

My heart beat so loudly I was sure they could hear it. I spoke, hoping to cover the thumping. I also wanted to change the subject.

"Whatever happened to the Watkins' property?" I asked.

"That's a legal question. You should ask Lettie's old friend, Colin Brinkley. He was a practicing lawyer then—

one of only two or three in the area. If he doesn't know what happened, he'll be able to direct you to someone who does."

"Coffee?" Judy asked.

"Yes, please, or I'm the one who might need to call my old friend, Judge Brinkley. I don't dare drive after drinking this amazing Chardonnay. If I were a betting man, my money would be on it as a winner this year."

"That was one of Aunt Lettie's dreams. I'd love for it to come true," I said. "With so many vintners entering the competition, it's a tough field."

We moved indoors, and as Judy and Vernon began asking each other questions about friends I didn't know, I gave them both hugs. "I'm going to do what you suggested and call Colin Brinkley. Thanks again for lunch and for the life lessons, too."

"Call me anytime if you have questions about Billie," he said as I headed to the reading room to call Judge Brinkley.

"Judge Brinkley," I said when the call went through.

"Yes?"

"It's Lily, Lily Callahan. I can't believe you're in your office on a Saturday. And during a holiday weekend!"

"If I didn't come in on Saturdays, I'd never get caught up. Holiday weekends are even quieter. What can I do for you?"

14

Property Matters

"FIRST, THANKS FOR helping us with Billie Dundee. He's a remarkable boy."

"Lettie used those very words to describe you at about his age. When all this trouble settles down, why don't you invite me over so we can reminisce about her? I have some stories to tell you about her that I bet you've never heard. She was a remarkable woman."

"I'd love that! I'm not sure I could have done it right after she died, but it would mean so much to me to hear more about her. I did my best to coax stories from her, but she never liked to talk about herself."

"Let's do it—soon. I'll bring a photo album I have with pictures from a trip we took together to the Middle East after the Arab-Israeli War. She didn't tell you about that, did she?"

"No, she did not, but I knew the two of you were close."

"Unfortunately for me, it was all perfectly innocent. Lettie wanted to visit the pyramids and other ancient landmarks before they were destroyed. She needed a male escort to accompany her to many of the places she wanted to go to in Arab countries. We kept it all very hush-hush since we traveled together. Lettie was afraid I'd never end up as a judge if the locals got wind of it." He sighed.

"My relationship with Lettie isn't the reason for your call. I'm sorry about the trouble at your place. I suspected there was more going on with Penney Lincoln and her family. Don't share this with anyone, but even though I represented Rachel and her husband, I wasn't sure Bud Lincoln didn't have something to do with Penney's disappearance."

"You thought he'd killed her?"

"No. If that were it, I'd have shared my suspicions with the police. I worried that he and Rachel knew more about her disappearance than they were willing to say, or they wouldn't have hired me. Some of the questions they asked were odd. I'd better leave it at that since I'm still bound by attorney-client privilege, although Bud passed on a few years ago."

"Well, I have a question about an entirely different matter. It's about the Watkins' property. Doctor Kennedy was here today giving Billie a checkup, and he said there was a terrible fire there years ago. He didn't believe anyone survived other than a five-year-old boy who was badly burned. Dustin Watkins was sent to San Francisco for care, and I wondered if he later inherited the property?"

"That was a long time ago—the place burned to the ground in the late seventies or early eighties. I'm sure Vernon told you about the Wappo Curse. I don't believe provisions were made for anyone to inherit the property.

My friend Sam Dickerson was more involved in estate planning, tax, and property matters than I was, but, sadly, he's no longer with us."

"Would it have been sold?"

"Not right away, I'm sure. No one would have been holding their breath waiting to get their hands on it. It wasn't cursed, but the land was flat and dry except where it backed up into the woods. There's an outcropping of granite, boulders, and a spring that's somehow tied to the Wappo Curse. It's likely the county eventually sold it for back taxes. The owner's name should be on a deed in the Recorder's Office. Do you want me to have a clerk find out who that is?"

"I hadn't even thought about looking for information about the property in the county tax records. If someone owns it, and is keeping up with the taxes, the information should be available online."

"If you run into trouble, tell me, and I'll help. Of course, if this is related to the bodies found on your property, Dahlia and Rikki are probably after the same information, aren't they?"

"They're not too interested in what I have to say, but I'll get the information to them. Hopefully, they won't bug you again if you decide to take a day off tomorrow."

"Lettie would tell you to keep on good terms with the law, even if you don't always play by the rules." He laughed. "Don't forget your promise to sit and talk about more pleasant topics."

"As soon as possible. I want you to meet Billie, too." I ended the call and figured there was no time like the present to look up the Watkins property. I had to dig up an address or a parcel number to search for it. Suddenly, I heard laughter and Billie burst into the room.

"Good job, Marlowe. He really is a detective. I told him to find Lily and he went straight to you from where we were above the garage. I'm supposed to fetch you for help. We need stuff for the sets—big stuff—but how are we going to get it here since we're grounded?"

"I guess we can't put it off much longer, can we?" When Billie said, "big stuff," he meant materials for the backdrops that would be used to create the illusion that we were on the set of Not Another Day. Or in this case, Not Another Day, Please!

Given the short time frame in which we had to work, we'd decided our first theatrical production would be a parody of the soap opera in which Melody and I had performed for so many years. Zelda could not only do hair and makeup, but her comic timing made her perfect as Andra's rival for the same man's affections. In true farce fashion, they both had different men in mind, and neither of the men was interested in Andra or Zelda who'd suggested we use her real name in the play—"with a cast of characters from A to Z," or some line like close to that.

Melody's character also had a problem. The two men Andra and Zelda had their eyes on were pursuing her, and she couldn't drive either of them away. We'd recruited two very funny friends to play the men's parts. The whole set up made for a modern version of A Midsummer Night's Dream merry mix up among star-crossed lovers with a few twists.

Julie had written many of the scripts in which Melody and I had performed, and she'd often played jokes on us during read-throughs by replacing the real dialogue with funny bits. We cut her loose to come up with a script. Julie called right away to get a release from the producers to make sure no one would give us grief about poking fun at our characters. The show was on its last legs anyway, so no one much cared., but I still had her get a release in writing.

"Finding a way to haul in the "big stuff" would be a problem even if we weren't grounded. Let's go! We'll come up with something."

We had an easier time of figuring out the smaller items we still needed to set up the sets. I had lots of unused furniture stored—an entire garage full. Rugs, lamps, paintings, and other accessories.

We'd figured out what to use for the main setting in which most of the action would take place. A living room with a front door and several other doors for characters to enter and exit, would be perfect for creating confusion. Especially for the hapless gentlemen who would be summoned and then hidden or dismissed by one of three women always seemingly on the verge of hysteria.

"I'll see if our jailers will let us start hauling these items over to the stage," I offered. "We can store some of the stuff in the basement if it doesn't all fit well enough in the storeroom backstage or in one of the dressing rooms we're not going to need."

"So that brings us back to the problem of what to do for backdrops. We don't need more than two or three change ups," Carrie said. "They should look as much like the ones used on the show as possible."

"We need the artist's renderings to fill in the details,

don't we? I should have already asked for those." Julie was on the phone in a flash. She was spoke to someone for several minutes as she paced around. Then she came running to where we had spread out the set designs Carrie had sketched for us.

"Are you sure? Squee! Hang on, Mick while I tell them!"

"Mick Daley just lost his job, isn't that great?" Julie asked.

"Does he feel that way about it?" I asked.

"He will if we hire him for a few months as our set designer and director. Get this, he also says if we pay to have them hauled up here, he can bring several of his old sets from the show's previous seasons."

I'm still not used to having money, so my stomach automatically cramps up when I'm considering major costs like hiring a set designer. When we'd roughed out a budget, sets had been one of the biggest ticket items in it. That's not saying much since we're all working for free, although I'd forbidden the divas from paying a cent toward room and board. I was still ruminating when Julie spoke.

"I'll tell him twenty dollars per hour—full-time work for the rest of the year," Julie suggested. "Plus, room and board until he can find a place to live."

"That's good for him since he's got no job and good for us since he actually knows what he's doing." Zelda was emphatic.

I tried to imagine where we'd put him. Two of my friends were already sharing the two-bedroom apartment over the garage, and the others were in suites on the second floor. Since Billie now occupied Lettie's suite that was usually Judy's room, she no longer had a room. Melody read my mind.

"Mick can sleep in the lounge on the second floor if we take the love seat out and move in a bed. It's got a nice bathroom with a great shower." Melody paused and then continued after a moment.

"Here's an even better idea. Let's put Billie in there and give Judy back her room. Then we'll haul your old bedroom set to the theater building and set it up for Mick in one of the small rehearsal rooms in the basement. It doesn't stink down there, and the room has a window to let in natural light. He won't have a private bathroom, but he can use the big one that's down there."

"There's already a mini fridge, microwave, and coffee pot down. What else does he need if he eats meals with us?" Zelda asked.

"Mick's going to spend most of his time in the theater building for the next few weeks, so why not arrange it that way?" Carrie added.

"Billie, is it okay with you if we move you to a different room?" I asked, wondering if it would make a difference to Diane.

"I'd love to live in the theater basement!" He clapped his hands. Then he stopped joking around. "The room down the hall is fine, too."

"You'll need more than a bed. We'll have to redecorate the room. It's way too girlie for you," I added. Once the money starts flowing, I can always come up with more ways to spend it.

"Yes! Carrie has baseball stuff we can use. I'm going to

go tell Judy she's getting her room back. Want me to bring up some chips?"

"No, we'll be down for dinner as soon as we work this out," I replied. Billie, Marlowe, and Darjeeling ran. It only took a few more seconds to realize this could give us the boost we needed to make up for time we'd lost.

"Offer him the deal and see what he says," I said. "Yes, to bringing the old sets with him. I don't know what kind of truck he needs, so he should figure it out and let me know where to send a check if they ask him for a deposit."

"Mick, here's the deal." Julie told him what we had in mind and he hardly let her finish before jumping at the chance. "He wants to know how soon he can start. Mick's living on his brother's couch, and his sister-in-law's not happy about it."

"Tell him he's on the clock now. As soon as he can arrange to have the sets moved, he should drive on up here." Then I considered the non-theater-related issues that dogged us. "Before he loads up his car, maybe you should let him know about our other messy issues." Zelda shook her head no, but Carrie nodded yes. It didn't matter because Julie was already spilling the beans.

"Uh, Mick before you pack up your car, there is one teeny-weeny glitch in all this." I wouldn't have used the teeny-weeny words, and technically, it's more than a glitch, but what the heck? "Messy issues" was an understatement too. Julie knows Mick better than I do.

"We're mixed up in some murder investigations and there are cops all over the vineyard property. It might not be over when you get here." Julie turned her back to us and I heard her whisper, "Six." Then she just listened for a couple of minutes.

"Uh-huh, I understand. Yep. Okay, call me as soon as you figure it out."

"Is he thinking about it?" I asked.

"No. He's on his way. Mick says that every time his sister-in-law picks up a kitchen knife, he's sure she's going to kill him in his sleep. His car is all packed. As soon as he can locate someone at the warehouse, he's going to have a moving van load up the sets, his tools, and a few other things like that. Mick says he can talk the movers into accepting payment at this end."

Everyone was still buzzing with excitement when we headed downstairs. The discussion continued through dinner about the decision we'd made to hire Mick and rearrange the rooms. Billie was excited about what to do with his room.

It wasn't until after dinner that I managed to find out more about the Watkins property. It took me some effort to locate the parcel and get an address. Once I had that, the public records were easy to find. There was an owner, but it was an LLC and not an individual. The price paid for the property was ridiculously low when the LLC bought it in 1985. Colin Brinkley had to be correct when he guessed it was sold for back taxes.

I also found a picture that must have appeared in a local paper. The husk of a barn—half a barn really—was all that remained standing. A pile of charred debris that must once have been Dustin's house lay near the frame of a burned-out car. The caption read, *Deadly Curse Strikes Again*, but I couldn't find an article that went with the photo.

I searched for news about the fire, hoping to find that an investigation had determined what caused it or more details about the Watkins family and a boy who survived the fire. I also searched for later references to the Watkins property, and found one mention that the large parcel of land was for sale with a note that all structures were destroyed by fire in 1980. It shouldn't have been frustrating that I found so little on the Internet since the fire had occurred before the Internet was publicly available or widely used.

I left a voice mail for Diane Constantine giving her Dustin's last name and the date the fire occurred. If someone from Children's Services had been contacted while he was at the local hospital, I hoped Diane could find out where Dustin Watkins had been placed once he'd recovered enough to be released from the hospital in San Francisco. I quickly learned that medical records don't have to be stored for more than seven years, so even if I knew which hospital in San Francisco had treated Dustin, I wasn't likely to find much.

I called Austin to tell him what we'd learned from our conversations with Doctor Kennedy and Judge Brinkley. It didn't escape my weary mind that hearing Austin's voice perked me up. He's a naturally funny guy—not only the hokey cowboy routine—but he finds humor in the world where I just don't see it.

His chats with locals in a community where a prison is the number one employer were upbeat. Only Austin could have forged a bond with a fugitive while returning him to face a prison sentence. Who knew what he'd learn from a man the prison guards refer to as Little Bigmouth?

"That's *Chief* Little Bigmouth to you, he told them," Austin said. "What a guy!"

"Why do they call him Little Bigmouth?" I asked.

"He's short and wiry but has a booming voice."

"Does Chief mean he's Native American?"

"Yes, but I never heard him refer to the Wappo tribe as his ancestors, if that's what you're getting at. To be honest, I can't remember what he said about his tribal affiliation."

"Maybe he's heard of the Wappo curse. Even if he's not from around here, he was in Calistoga when he spoke to the police about Penney Lincoln."

"I'll ask him. From what he told the police, he wasn't in town when he saw Penney Lincoln. If he gave the police more details about exactly where he was, it's not in the written record. I can't believe he wouldn't have made a point of telling them that the man speaking to Penney Lincoln had a face scarred from burns."

"You said he was trying to play let's make a deal with the police. Who knows what he kept to himself?"

"True. You must be exhausted, Lily. Get some sleep. I won't be around to beg you to come downstairs in the middle of the night after locking myself out." I suddenly felt a rush of warmth at the memory of that embrace. "You were an awfully good sport about it."

"I haven't always been such a good sport, have I?" I held up my hand and examined the ring on my finger. "I promise to try harder to be less afraid and cynical. Romance was as phony as all the air kisses and double-edged compliments doled out in Hollywood. I'm a mess. I admit it."

"That doesn't bother me. I never cared much about being alone before we met, and I miss you every minute. Just promise that you'll be my mess, okay?"

I have no idea where his earnestness and willingness to trust came from. His life was no bed of roses growing up. Lawmen see the worst of what people do to each other—including broken promises by couples who'd vowed to love and cherish each other forever. I wished he were here with me so I could try again to discover the secret of his courage and strength.

"I miss you, too, and I'm your mess as long as you can stand it." And if the messes in my life don't get either one of us killed. "Call me tomorrow when you're on your way home."

"Will do, Lily." As I said goodnight, I was trembling. There's something in the way Austin says my name that's more tender and romantic than all the other sweet words I've ever heard combined. How is that possible?

15

Faint or Feint?

Brandy Lewis was, indeed, a big girl. She towered over Billie and stood toe-to-toe with me. Her parents were even taller. They were polite, although clearly anxious about meeting with the police. I'd bet they hadn't expected to spend their Sunday morning chatting over coffee with the police. We were barred from the room as soon as we'd made the family comfortable with beverages and a plate of cookies.

I'd tried to take Dahlia aside and tell her what we'd learned from Dr. Kennedy and what Judge Brinkley told me. I got a hand in my face for my trouble. My gesture was simply an attempt to be courteous. I had to assume that if Austin considered the information important to the investigation, he'd relay it to Rikki.

When the interview was over, Brandy was visibly shaken. I assumed that meant she'd been told about her teacher's death. I wondered if the best thing for her to do was to leave right away for the comfort of home, but a promise is a promise, so I didn't want to be the one to suggest it to her.

"I'm going to have Jim Brady accompany you to the theater," Dahlia announced in an officious tone. "Please stay together, and if you have questions, ask Officer Brady."

"Do you have a background in the theater, too?" Ms. Lewis asked Jim Brady in a naïve tone. Brandy rolled her eyes, and then Ms. Lewis sent me a sideways glance, smirking. Jim tried to hide his amusement since he was onto her.

"All the world is a stage, is it not?" Jim asked as he spread his arm wide, opened the front door, and led us out onto the porch.

"Nicely put, Jim," Mr. Lewis murmured as he followed me out of the house. "I was worried the missus was going to fly over the table a time or two. She does not appreciate anyone needlessly upsetting Brandy."

"To be honest, my colleague isn't always the most skilled interviewer. In this case, she knew Brandy's teacher, so she's having a harder time staying on an even keel."

I wondered what Jim meant by that. Neither of the men seemed to mind that I was listening in on their conversation, so I continued to walk with them hoping to learn as much as I could. Mrs. Lewis was walking ahead of us talking to Judy.

Billie and Brandy walked side by side, with Brandy carrying Marlowe. Billie had insisted that Brandy carry our "comfort pooch." I'm sure that term had come from Melody, who, on more than one occasion, had been allowed into stores with Darjeeling in her purse. The rest of my friends were told to stay behind. Hostages, I guess, in case we tried to make our escape.

"Isn't she supposed to recuse herself or something like that if it's personal?" Mr. Lewis asked.

"I don't mean it's personal in that way," Jim responded.

"Was it something about Brandy? She was like a Doberman with a cat cornered up a tree when she questioned her." Mr. Lewis turned to me.

"No offense, I'm not talking about your little fella. He's a good dog with so many strangers in the house."

"No offense, taken. I think what Jim is trying to say is that Dahlia's behavior *isn't* about Brandy, but maybe it ought to be. Brandy's young and she was closer to her teacher than your colleague, Jim." Something about what I said must have upset Jim because I saw his jaw tighten. Was he worried Brandy's parents would file a complaint against the department? It wasn't his fault.

"Let's hope we can make it up to Brandy. I'm sure she was a big help to the investigation."

"She did her best, but she's a student, not her teacher's confidant. It's not her fault she doesn't know the name of the man her teacher's dating—was dating. It's a crying shame that a wonderful person like Ms. Wainwright is dead. I hope they find the miserable so and so. Brandy can't be the only one who saw her get into that souped-up Camaro."

I stumbled and Jim took my arm to steady me. When I made eye contact with him, he nodded yes to my unuttered question—was the car black? A sighting of someone in a black Camaro picking up another victim made it a little easier to understand why Dahlia had pushed Brandy so hard.

When we stepped through the trees onto the theater grounds, Brandy squealed with excitement. She put Marlowe down as she and Billie ran down the middle aisle.

"It's bigger than I thought it would be!"

"Let's go up on stage, Brandy. We'll sing something." They were on the stage in a flash and stepped centerstage. For a moment, they discussed what to sing. Brandy giggled, nodded, and they launched into an acapella version of *Ebony and Ivory*. They were surprisingly good, and the difference in their heights was adorable. By the way they worked in a few dance steps, this couldn't have been entirely improvised.

"Have they performed this song before?" I asked Mr. Lewis.

"Brandy sang the song with someone else last year for the students in Ms. Wainwright's class. Billie must have paid close attention. He's got most of the moves down."

"Brandy's got star quality written all over her. Their voices are great together," I added, cheering as they bowed. Then I put my fingers in my mouth and whistled the way Aunt Lettie had taught me to do.

"Warn me next time you plan to do that!" Mr. Lewis said as he wiggled his ear and laughed.

"It's a deal! Let's go congratulate the stars." I took off running for the stairs that led up to the stage, cheering all the way.

"That was awesome, you two!" I exclaimed when I reached them. "Brandy you have a great voice." She curtsied.

"Thank you." Then Brandy hugged me.

"You do too, Billie! Why didn't you tell us you could sing?"

"Nobody asked me," he said. I ruffled his hair, and it stood up on end.

"How would you like to do that in front of a bigger audience?" I was suddenly inspired to include them in our opening night.

"Singing's not in the show," Billie commented. "Where would it go?"

"I don't know," I said. "That's for our writer to figure out. Let's go backstage." For almost an hour, we set aside worries about murder and mayhem, although I did check that all the windows were closed in the basement. When I returned to the stage with Billie and Brandy, her mother was sitting and chatting with Judy. Jim and Brandy's dad were doing the same thing, closer to the stage.

"These seats are comfortable," Mr. Lewis commented as he stood.

"That's good, Dad, because Billie and I are going to be in the show here during the Thanksgiving Harvest Festival."

"You are?" her mother asked as she stood, too.

"If it's okay with you two, of course," I added. "I'm not even sure exactly what they'll do, but a duet of some kind."

"It's going to be a big audience. Are ready for that, Brandy?" her mother asked.

"Definitely!"

"Then why not?" Billie and Brandy hooted and hollered. They hammed it up doing a silly dance routine onstage.

"What are you doing?" A thin, middle-aged woman asked as she squeezed through the trees not far from the steps leading up to the stage.

"Time to go," Jim said immediately. He stood up and stepped closer to the woman. I motioned for Billie and Brandy to come down from the stage, and, in seconds, we were standing with Brandy's parents.

"Mrs. Lincoln, where are you?" That was Dahlia's voice.

"Mr. and Mrs. Lewis why don't you and the kids go back to the house with Judy while Jim and I reunite Mrs. Lincoln with Dahlia?" Judy herded everyone together and ushered them up the aisle toward the main exit. I saw Judy waving at someone who must have been Dahlia.

"Mrs. Lincoln, I'm Lily Callahan. Would you like me to show you around the theater building?" Jim inched closer to Mrs. Lincoln and reached for her arm. She dashed up the stairs to the stage.

"Don't let me stop the party!" she shouted. Judy and the others were gone, but Dahlia and Rikki came running toward us. Mrs. Lincoln spun around on stage. Was she drunk? She hadn't reeked of alcohol like Billie's mother. Drugs maybe?

"Mrs. Lincoln, I can tell you're upset. What can I do?" I asked as I slowly walked up each step until I was on stage with her.

"Why not invite more people to dance on my daughter's grave?" Penney's mom opened her arms as if she were standing in front of an audience.

"I understand how stressful it must be to find out that Penney's dead. It was shocking to me and I was a friend, not her mother."

"Don't lie to me. Penney didn't have any friends." She stopped and stared at me. "Especially not a snooty girl like you."

"I was new in school at the time, but she was friendly toward me. She was cute and funny and appeared to have plenty of friends."

"Boyfriends—that's what you mean, don't you? The police told me they'd heard that, and I told them whoever said it was lying. I didn't want them to believe I was a bad mother." The woman began to sob. My eyes filled with tears as I went to her and put my arms around her. Jim moved closer to the steps.

"I'm sure you did your best. It's not your fault Penney got mixed up with the wrong person. I'm sorry."

"You're acting, Lily Callahan. If I'd told the police someone had picked her up, she might still be alive, but Bud said it would make me look bad since I didn't even know who it was. Penney and I had another fight about her stepfather telling her what to do. I thought she'd run off like she'd done before. Penney was gone for three days before I called the police and asked them to look for her." She pulled away from me and scanned the area around the theater as if searching for an escape route.

"I knew no high school kid could afford a hot car like that. When I asked who was picking her up, Penney told me a parent was driving and his daughter was in the car, too."

The more she rambled on, the more confused I became about her story. If Penney didn't have friends, why was it so easy for her to believe a friend's parent was picking them up in a black Camaro? It had to be the same car Jesse had seen picking up Penney at school. Had Mrs. Lincoln seen it before?

Why was she convinced that Penney had run away if she'd left the house with a friend and her parent? Had Penney given her the name of the friend, and had her mother tried to locate Penney at the friend's house?

"Let's go inside where it's quiet. I'll tell the police to keep out, and we'll sit and talk with coffee or a glass of wine." A smile flitted across her face.

"Is that okay with you?" She asked Jim and the two women standing at the foot of the stairs on opposite sides of the stage. Then Mrs. Lincoln looked up for a second and turned as white as a ghost before crumpling to the ground. When I glanced in the direction she'd been looking, I caught a glimmer of light, as if the sun had reflected off a shiny object. Had it been the decorative lights strung up in the trees glinting in the sunlight or had she seen something—or someone—else?

"There!" I pointed and Jim took off. Dahlia was speaking into a mic.

"Don't touch her!" she ordered as I knelt beside Mrs. Lincoln. "I ordered an ambulance and EMTs. I understand something like this happened last night when Jim and another officer went to her house to tell her we'd found her daughter's body. They took her to the ER and, by her behavior today, I'm assuming she was given some heavy-duty medications. Wine would not have been a good idea."

"What was she doing here if you knew she wasn't well?" I asked.

"She wanted to see where we found her daughter's body, and we want her to tell us which of several items we found belonged to her daughter."

"Why put her through that if what she wanted to do was visit the site where her daughter had been buried all these years?"

"You know why," Dahlia snapped. "We're trying to keep the lid on this mess." Rikki had come up on stage.

"What Dahlia means is it's the same reason we interviewed Brandy and her family here. We're hoping to protect Rachel Lincoln's privacy and the rest of the family members involved in this terrible ordeal." Rikki knelt beside the woman who hadn't moved since she hit the stage floor.

"Since you've decided we're all a bunch of conspirators, that's not such a good idea."

"I'm sorry I lost my cool yesterday. It's not just your privacy we're concerned about. If you believe what Dustin told you, you're a target, Lily, and the Sitter's a very dangerous man." Mrs. Lincoln stirred as Rikki took her pulse. I leaned in as Rachel Lincoln murmured.

"Too old for a sitter," is what I was almost certain she said. Rikki wasn't paying attention as EMTs came racing toward us.

"That was quick. I didn't hear an ambulance," I said as I scooted out of the way so they could examine Mrs. Lincoln. I hadn't realized that her hand was touching me. When I moved, she roused from her stupor and reached for me. I bent down and squeezed her hand, and then Rikki and I left the stage.

"After what went on with the elusive Numbers Man

yesterday, Dahlia put one on call in the winery parking lot across the road."

"You can do that?" I asked.

"We share rescue vehicles with the Fire Department," Dahlia responded. "If they needed it for an emergency, they could still use it."

"From what Austin told us about the fire at the Watkins' place, we've also got a fire truck on standby. Thanks for getting the information to us. You could have called me directly, though. I wish you would, Lily. Even minutes might make a difference with a man like the Sitter."

"I hear you, Rikki. Brandy's dad said she couldn't tell you much about Ms. Wainwright's boyfriend. According to Billie, there were a couple of men at the school when he ran into her. Since you're still asking questions about who Brandy's teacher was seeing, I take it she wasn't there to meet either of them?"

"I wish that had been the case. They both gave us alibis for the evening Ms. Wainwright was killed. Before you ask, yes, she was there for a meeting with the choir instructor—a woman, not a man."

I nodded. It made me a little sad to think that they might have been there to plan another performance by Brandy and her classmates for Ms. Wainwrights' sixth-graders.

"Her sister was wrong if Ms. Wainwright was making plans as if she expected to be teaching rather than packing her bags for a Vegas wedding and Hawaii honeymoon." I was mostly talking to myself. Rambling really when another question suddenly seemed important to ask. "Rikki, when you and Dahlia spoke to Mrs. Lincoln earlier, did you ask her if she'd ever had a sitter for her daughter?"

"We asked her generally about supervision, but not specifically about a sitter. Why?" I repeated Rachel Lincoln's words for the two policewomen.

"I guess she could have thought we were asking her a question about a sitter for Penney when she heard me say 'sitter.' She was out of it," Rikki shrugged.

"Either that or she's deliberately trying to be evasive. Do you believe the drama you just witnessed onstage?" Jim joined us as Dahlia asked that question.

"I had trouble following some of her rant, and there were contradictions in what she said. She admitted she'd seen the same black Camaro Jesse saw Penney get into out in front of her school, but I couldn't understand why she believed Penney was leaving with a friend and her parent, or if she was saying that was the last time that she ever saw her daughter."

"That's what I'm talking about," Dahlia said. "We tried several times to get her to clarify issues like that before she took off. What's not clear to me is if she's confused or holding out on us. The confusion could be an act. Why doesn't she want to do everything in her power to help find the killer? Passing out on stage got her out of here, didn't it?"

"Rikki can tell you that Rachel Lincoln was out cold, so I don't believe she was faking it. The fear on her face seemed real too. What could she have seen that scared her?"

"Nothing as far as we can determine," Jim replied. "We searched the entire area. There wasn't a soul around other than the police officers on duty today. Members of the crime scene cleanup crew are all accounted for, and there's only one investigator at each dumpsite to oversee the cleanup in case they missed something while collecting the evidence. Jesse says he and his field hands were in a completely different area of the vineyard. So, there's no obvious explanation for what caused her to faint."

"By that, do you mean faint as in pass out or feint as in create a deception to distract us?" I shook my head and waved goodbye giving Dahlia the last word.

Dahlia could be right that Mrs. Lincoln still wasn't being completely truthful, but why not? Or maybe the fainting spell was related to a medical problem or the drugs prescribed for her at the hospital last night as Dahlia had also suggested. I could have been wrong to assume she was staring at something in the distance. Last night, Doctor Kennedy had appeared to be looking at the horizon when, in fact, he was peering into the past. Had an old memory or a new revelation been responsible for Mrs. Lincoln's swoon?

16

Another Lincoln

THE LEWIS FAMILY had departed by the time I walked into the kitchen. Judy was still in the process of explaining all that had gone on to those who'd missed the events. I was glad to hear that Billie and Brandy had been so excited about being part of the opening night show, they'd hardly mentioned Rachel Lincoln's dramatic entry. They'd missed her fainting spell, although when the ambulance left, the driver had used the sirens. Judy had explained that Mrs. Lincoln must have become ill and was being taken to the hospital.

Billie had gone upstairs to put away his clothes and schoolbooks. Jim Brady had dropped them off before he'd escorted us to the theater. I'd snooped through Billie's belongings, hoping his notebook was among them. No such luck. If they'd found the notebook, the police already had it.

I filled everyone in on what had gone on after Judy left. They all agreed that Rachel Lincoln had to be distressed about her daughter's death. Judy and my diva pals also had no qualms about insisting that Penney's mother was hiding something—maybe the same something that had her frightened out of her wits. Zelda was emphatic.

"Mrs. Lincoln can't pretend anymore; she knows what happened to her daughter. She's not just scared, but atterorizado!"

"What's that mean?" Billie asked as he bolted into the kitchen in worn jeans and a baseball jersey that was a size too large for him.

"Terrified," Zelda responded. Then she threw her arms up and made a face as if she was scared. "Like Andra Weis will be in our play."

"What should we have for lunch?" I asked, redirecting the conversation to a more pleasant topic. I admired the smooth way in which Zelda had avoided lying to Billie without having to go into the details about Penney Lincoln's fate.

In all the excitement of the morning, I hadn't worried too much about the fact that Austin hadn't called yet. I wanted him to call so I could hear what he'd learned, but I also wanted to find out when he'd be home. Now that things had quieted down, I began to worry. I called him, but his phone was switched off.

I kept busy by making a list of all the grocery items we needed. Unless we were set free soon, I'd have to get Doctor Kennedy to send Jim Brady shopping for us. He'd need a truck to do that at the rate we were eating our way through everything in the pantry, freezer, and fridge.

When my phone rang, I grabbed it. Someone pounded on the backdoor, and Carrie dashed to open it. The angry look on Jesse's face softened when Carrie smiled at him.

"Hello, Austin," I said as Jesse stepped inside and

greeted Carrie. Despite Carrie's soothing effect, Jesse was still all worked up.

"What the heck is wrong with that woman?" Jesse bellowed.

"What woman?" Austin asked. We had an echo in the house as Melody and Zelda asked Jesse the same question.

"I think Jesse's asking about Rachel Lincoln. She showed up here, escaped from Dahlia and Rikki, and then pitched a fit before passing out center stage. The EMTs hauled her away to the ER in an ambulance." Then Billie rushed into the kitchen with the dogs.

"Lily, Marshal Rikki's at the front door. She needs to speak to you."

"Thanks, Billie. Please tell her I'll be right there." I hadn't heard the doorbell ring or seen Billie leave the kitchen, so I'd missed my chance to hide.

"As you heard, I've been summoned to the front door. Can you all answer Jesse's questions about what happened to Rachel Lincoln?"

"Austin, did you call to warn me Rikki's ticked off with me about something? She told me I should call her directly rather than passing information to you first, but she didn't seem mad at me." I hustled down the hallway as I spoke to Austin.

"No. In fact, she said the information you got from Dr. Kennedy was helpful. Dahlia already sent a team of officers to the Watkins' place to see if there's anywhere Dustin could be hiding."

"That's good, I take it they didn't find anything, or you'd be more excited than you are."

"I haven't heard anything from them one way or another. You've had a busy morning. Did Brandy Lewis and her parents show up too?"

"Yes. I've got plenty to tell you about their visit. Some of it's even happy if you can believe that. First, I got to see what I've done to perturb my jailers."

"Yes, Rikki, what can I do for you?" I asked.

"Are you expecting a delivery? There's a moving van at the gate and a guy following him in a car that shouldn't be on the highway as jampacked as it is. He says he's not afraid of a serial killer, so we should let him onto the property."

"Gosh, he got here quick. That's our set designer, Mick Daley. The sets are in the van. Let them in, please and tell them to turn off onto the road leading to the theater."

"I'm not a traffic cop. What I should do is turn them away." Until then, I hadn't noticed that Dahlia was standing on the porch, off to one side. It wasn't her words, but the condescending tone in her voice that set my teeth on edge. She couldn't have made me cringe more if she'd scraped her fingernails across a blackboard.

"Are you kidding me? This is private property. I get to say who comes and goes. In fact, Dahlia, you've had all the time you get to pretend you're running the Calla Lily Vineyards. They're cleaning up the slime pit, so I don't see why you even need to remain on my property. I want you and all your equipment out of the vineyards by midnight tonight. That also goes for the winery property. If you still need to get into the woods, ask one of the other property owners around here to help you out. Better yet, there must be a public access road somewhere, find it, and use it."

"Jesse!" I shouted. He came running with an entourage following him. "Will you call the gate and tell whoever's time is being wasted by the police to let the moving van and the car behind the van in through the gates? Tell them to turn off onto the road leading to the theater and follow the signs for deliveries."

"Just so it's clear, she's the woman I was talking about, not Rachel Lincoln." Jesse was on his phone as he pointed at Dahlia. It took twenty seconds to end the standoff at the vineyard gates. "After we spent almost an hour searching for a nonexistent intruder, Dahlia made me do a roll call. She checked every man on the work roster. We're at least a couple of hours behind."

"Are you getting all this?" I asked Austin, turning away while Jesse vented.

"Most of it. Just once, I'd like to call you without a knock-down-drag-out battle going on in the background."

"You and me both," I replied.

Dahlia was about to protest. I have no idea what she planned to say because it no longer mattered. Apparently, Rikki didn't want to hear it, either. She put out an arm to keep Dahlia from stepping forward.

"If you'll let me speak, the main reason I came here was to tell you that we're clearing out at the end of the day," Rikki said. "I'm still advising you to take extra precautions given the points you just made about the gaps in security. You've got your friends and the child to worry about now."

"I agree, Rikki. I know you mean well. I'll call my security consultant and see what else we can do. We're going to be open to the public soon, so I don't want it to look like an armed camp. If you want us all to be safe, find the killer." I didn't slam the door, but I did shut it.

"Let's all go meet Mick. Julie, will you make sure Mick parks near the door that leads straight into the basement? He'll avoid most of the stairs that way. I'm going to lock up the house, and then I'll be right there to see if I can talk the movers into hauling the stuff from the garage over there." When everyone stood there, Judy spoke up.

"We're free to go, people." That snapped everyone out of it.

"Jesse, I know you're incredibly busy, but you should go with us, so we can introduce you to Mick Daley. He's going to be here the rest of the year." She took his arm. "You heard what Rikki said about gaps in security, we need you to come with us."

"Does that mean you're going to be around until the end of the year, too?" He asked.

"I don't see why not. A Christmas in wine country would be fun, don't you think?" Carrie asked looking over her shoulder at the other divas. Melody rolled her eyes, and Zelda put her fingers together into the shape of a heart, making Billie snicker. When they all took off, I spoke to Austin as I locked the door in the kitchen.

"All clear, Austin!"

"Woo-wee, woman, remind me never to rile you up like that!"

"It's taken several days before I finally lost it. Well, lost it again since you put an end to mudwrestling in the slime pit. They can't say I didn't try since then. What is it about Dahlia? Does she hate me because I love you?"

Oops. Did I just say that? Austin was silent.

"I love you too. I wish I was there to show you how much, Fire Lily." I could see the smile on his face and the way he looked at me as though there was no one else in the world but me. I realized I'd taken a long pause.

"The sparks were flying, weren't they?" I asked.

"Here, too! I do love feisty!"

"So, you've said. That's good because there's plenty more where that came from, Cowboy," I said, in a teasing way that left him speechless. I giggled, and then restarted the conversation.

"What news do you have for me?" I asked as I slung my purse over my shoulder and tossed the keys into it after locking the front door. I searched around me, anxiously, as I hustled to catch up with the others.

"I've already texted the information to Rikki. Maybe Dahlia's upset because you're a step ahead of them even while they've had you under lock and key. Anyway, the Chief said he told the police that the homeless man had been burned in a fire."

"Then it had to be Dustin," I said, excited by his news. "Did your informant hear anyone call him by his name?"

"No, but this is interesting. The girl with him called him 'Rain Man.'"

"Like the character Dustin Hoffman played opposite Tom Cruise in the movie?" I asked.

"That's what the Chief figured. Maybe it was a play on the fact that his real name is Dustin and she knew it, or maybe it was her version of a name like the Numbers Man."

"That couldn't have been their first meeting if she knew him well enough to be aware of his interest in numbers, and to have a nickname for him."

"I agree. The Chief only saw him them together once, but Jesse saw Penney getting into the Camaro at school, so it's possible she'd met Dustin on at least one other occasion."

"Chief Little Bigmouth has a good memory for names."

"Penney' name stuck with the Chief because of the famous Lincoln penny, which is still popular among coin collectors. Stealing coins and other collectibles is among my pen pal's favorite targets. He stole a very valuable penny which is what landed him in prison—especially since he never returned it."

"His retirement plan, I assume. If he's ever released from prison."

"You could be right," Austin responded. "They tacked on more years for his escape, but he's been a model prisoner since then. Anyway, here's the information I wanted to pass along to you before I get home because it's related to the identity of the Sitter. The Chief claims Penney wasn't the only Lincoln talking to the homeless man that day. The Chief says he never saw the guy because he was behind the wheel of a shiny black Camaro yelling at Penney. Penney called him Uncle Link."

"Are you kidding me? If he was her uncle, that means he must have been her stepfather's brother, right? Can't they track him down using that information?"

"Bud Lincoln's dead and I hear his wife isn't in good shape, but Rikki's working on it."

"Why was Penney's Uncle Link yelling at her?" I asked.

"He was trying to make her get into the car, and she didn't want to do it."

"A teenager arguing with her uncle might not have seemed sinister to the police at the time. Especially if the uncle was concerned about the homeless guy talking to her. Surely, they would have checked with Bud and Rachel Lincoln."

I breathed a little easier now that I had caught up enough to hear my friends chattering and laughing up ahead. I didn't cut through the trees this time but continued down a road that led to the side lot where Mick and the movers would park.

"I can't believe they didn't at least ask Bud Lincoln about it. What the Chief told them next may could have convinced them not to take anything he said seriously. The Chief told them he 'sensed' that the man in the car was a cop."

"As in a 'sixth sense?'" I asked.

"Something like that. He couldn't explain it to them or to me. The driver wore black leather gloves, which lots of drivers other than cops, wear while driving. It was mainly an impression he got from the way the guy behind the wheel ordered them both around. In fact, he tells me that when he heard the girl was missing, he went to the police assuming Dustin was too."

"What does Rikki make of the Chief's suspicion that the driver was a cop?" I asked.

"She didn't dismiss the idea. Given that the murders have gone undetected for decades, a killer with knowledge of police protocols would have an edge. There aren't any Lincolns on the force, and no Lincolns besides Bud and

Rachel listed with addresses in the area. I know that because I spent a few minutes searching before I called Rikki."

"Shoot! That's too bad," I kicked the gravel with my shoe. "I was hoping Little Bigmouth had come up with a short cut to ending this miserable situation. I guess it was a good idea to kick the cops off the property, just in case the Chief is right, and the driver of the Camaro is a member of the police force. It's also possible, however, that Penney wasn't speaking to a real uncle, nor does 'Uncle Link' necessarily mean Lincoln."

"That's one of the first issues Rikki raised. She looked it up and L-i-n-k is a man's first name, although I've never known anyone who used it."

"It's an awfully big coincidence, though. If Penney left with her uncle, why wouldn't her mother have told the police that's who picked her up at the house? Today, when Dahlia asked her about the Camaro, she admitted Penney left in that car, but she told them one of Penney's friend's parents was behind the wheel. Could the car have been owned by a Lincoln without Rachel knowing it?"

"It doesn't seem likely, so maybe she's not willing to tell the truth."

"Why lie about it, Austin?"
"You said she was terrified. Maybe fear of retribution from the killer or fears that the police will suspect her of being involved in the murder of her daughter—especially if it turns out the killer is her husband's relative. This was a second marriage, so it's possible Rachel May become, didn't be known. all the check men speak to one, the Lincoln family."

huh?" A truck shifted into lower gear behind me. I turned to see the moving van lumbering toward me.

"I wouldn't say that. Having Dustin's name is progress, and we have a better description of him, as well as a possible connection between the Watkins and the Lincolns. Tying Dustin to that awful fire at the Watkins' place may also produce results. Rikki's trying to get a better understanding of what's on the property besides the old structures."

"Doesn't she need the current owner's permission to traipse around on their land?"

"The police made an emergency visit to make sure no one had broken in or was 'squatting' on the land. The possibility that a dangerous fugitive is hiding on the property won't allow them to stay put for long without a court order or permission from the owner. She's working on both angles. Trying to find out who owns the LLC that purchased the property is tricky."

"Good luck. One of the reasons people purchase properties using LLCs is so they can conceal their identities. Celebrities do that all the time, so they're not hounded by paparazzi or stalkers."

"I wish we could nail this guy, but it's a complicated case. It could take a while longer, which is why I already called Peter March and asked him to get here or send a couple of his security team members. You've got to kick it up another notch at the house and the theater at the very least."

"You heard me tell Rikki I'm ready to do more to keep us all safe," I said as I stepped off the roadway to make sure the moving van had plenty of room. The driver of the moving van pulled up alongside me and stopped.

"Are you the one with the money?" he asked.

"Give me a minute, will you?" I held up a finger.

"Here we go again, Austin. How far away are you?"

"I stopped to fill up the gas tank and call you. I'll be there in a couple of hours."

"Okay, drive carefully, but I'm taking everyone out to dinner now that we've been set free. Please get here in time to join us." Austin said goodbye, leaving me with a silly grin on my face. Until the mover spoke.

"Oh, yeah, you're the one with the money." I arched a brow and put a hand on my hip in response to the cheeky remark. He tucked his head back inside the truck.

"Pull into the lot and line up your truck with the stairs that lead up onto the stage—unless you've got a hoist." He gave me a blank look that I took to mean he didn't have a hoist.

"Stairs will cost you extra," he added as he pulled forward.

"Julie, do we have a hoist?" I hollered. She came running. As soon as the van pulled into the lot, Mick caught up with me and spotted Julie. He rolled his window down and stuck his head out while he kept driving.

"Julie! Hello, baby!" I ran ahead while she chatted with Mick as he continued to drive with his head and one arm out the window, gesturing wildly as he talked. At least he'd slowed down.

"Lily, Mick's got a hoist if we don't have one," Julie called out after me.

"Great!" I said as I searched for Billie and the dogs as the mover maneuvered his truck into place. Judy held onto the back of Billie's shirt, and he had both pooches on leashes. Thank goodness there was an adult in the group. Zelda, Melody, and Carrie were up on stage, doing fake gymnastics. I hoped they were fake, because if they weren't, they were so bad that we were going to need another ambulance any minute now.

Please don't let it be a new routine they were working on for the play, I thought. That reminded me that we needed the movers to haul furniture from the garage to the theater building. When I cornered the driver and spelled out what we wanted him to do, he agreed—for a price. I had finished the negotiations and written him a big fat check when I heard police sirens. Whoever was driving, was moving fast!

"If they hassle us again, that's going to cost you extra too, lady." The driver planted himself in the entrance to the parking lot with his arms folded across his chest. Dahlia screeched to a halt inches from him when she realized he wasn't going to budge.

"Lily, I don't have time to tangle with Goliath. Get into the car now, please. It's Rachel Lincoln. She's in the ER and wants to talk to you. I don't know how long they can keep her alive."

"Judy!" I ran.

"Go! We know what we're supposed to do. Don't worry. We can handle it."

"Hey! We need to get in there and turn around," I shouted to the mover who was scratching his head as I jumped into the front seat of Dahlia's patrol car.

"No, we don't," Dahlia said. "Buckle up." Dahlia put her car in reverse and gunned it. Gravel sprayed as we backed up to the intersection of gravel roads. She turned and headed back toward the paved road leading to the gate and hit the siren. I remember very little of the trip after that since I kept my eyes closed.

17

Dying Declaration

RACHEL LINCOLN HAD walked out of the ER without a release from the attending physician. She'd left her car at the vineyard, but the police had dropped it off for her in the visitor lot. Apparently, she had no trouble locating the car, but didn't get far before she ended up in a ditch.

"I'm sorry I had to intrude on your time with your sister," I said as I left the ICU and spotted Rachel's sister, Roslyn, who'd been in the room when Dahlia and I arrived. She hadn't been happy when the police asked her to step out of the room. In fact, she'd refused to do it until Rachel had spoken my name.

"I'm so sorry for her. I hope Rachel Lincoln makes it," I told Rikki as soon as Roslyn had gone back into Rachel's room.

"I'm sorry, too," Rikki said. "I don't know how anyone could have gotten help any quicker than she did given that she was only blocks away. Since the local police were already out on the road searching for her, they must have arrived at the crash site moments after she ran off the road."

Instead of being reassured, the fact that the police were searching for Rachel Lincoln, made my stomach knot up. If Austin's informant was correct that the driver of a black Camaro was a cop, who knows what had happened?

"Who found her car?" I asked.

"The guy who dropped it off for her here at the hospital. He's upset about it," Rikki replied.

"Could she really have been driving fast enough for the impact to have thrown her from the car?"

"Dahlia's at the accident scene now. Don't tell Dahlia I shared this with you, but if Rachel Lincoln dies, it'll be from a blow to the back of her head, which has nothing to do with her accident." I felt dizzy.

"It's the Sitter, isn't it?" Rikki answered my question with a shrug.

"I'd be a very bad cop to say yes without more evidence, but off-the-record, I believe it's him—whoever he is."

"Could the wound have been caused by a nightstick?"

"You mean because the killer is a police officer as Chief Little Bigmouth believes, who shared his story with another Deputy Bigmouth, who passed the story along to you?" Rikki asked.

Nabbed! I thought. When I didn't respond, Rikki shook her head.

"Let me buy you a coffee while we wait for Dahlia to return. If I'm speaking off-the-cuff about an investigation in which you're deeply involved, but not a pro, I ought to make a little effort to do it privately."

I followed Rikki through a door marked "Hospital Personnel." We poured coffee from a pot in a small lounge area. No one else was in the room when we sat down.

"I'm less certain about the killer being a police officer than I am about the Sitter possibly killing Rachel Lincoln. To answer your question, most officers carry retractable batons now since they're loaded up with so much gear. Those have a much narrower tip than what you're calling a nightstick."

"Could he be masquerading as a police officer to put his victims at ease?" I asked, suddenly recalling what Dustin had told us about the Sitter being a liar. "He might not know what kind of baton to carry if he's a pretender."

"If the murders were random, dressing up like a cop would make more sense to me as a quick way to gain a stranger's trust. The more we've learned, the more connected all the deaths seem to be. I'm not sure how or why," Rikki said as she sipped her coffee. "This is not to be repeated, but the third victim's DNA, a woman we still haven't identified, shares some characteristics in common with the mother and child."

"No! Another Watkins? I didn't know there were any other Watkins family members."

"None of this has been established yet."

"It does make this all appear to be connected, doesn't it?" I asked and then rushed on. "From the way the murders played out, I'd worked up a ritual killer scenario. You know—a murder around the same time of the year every decade, the ages of the victims getting older as if an aging killer chose a new victim close to his own age as he also grew older. Then poor broken Dustin is running around, spouting crazy things about numbers and watching the graves, so the bodies don't get out." I quit peering into my coffee cup as if the secret was hidden in the dark brew. When I looked up, Rikki was gazing at me with her mouth hanging open. "What? You're not buying the maniacal serial killer idea?"

"Please don't tell me Austin also shared information from the ME's office or details about the evidence the crime scene investigators have dug up—quite literally in this case?"

"Uh, no. Apart from the fact that I've lived through two of the murders, I also happened to see an email from Ben."

"Has he been gob smacked by your diva pal, Julie, like Austin has been by you?"

"To be honest, Dahlia left a printed copy of the email from Ben on my dining room table. If Austin or Ben were under our power, as you suggest, I'd already know more than I do, including the fact that a police baton wasn't the likely murder weapon. Although, now that you've told me the same weapon appears to have been used repeatedly since the first murder in 1979—that makes my sicko ritual killer idea a little stronger, doesn't it?"

"I'm in deep now, too, aren't I?" Rikki responded, shaking her head. "My take on the preliminary autopsy findings, is that whatever was used was more like a heavy flashlight. The first victim was a child killed forty years ago, so maybe it's a cop who's committed to his old school 'nightstick,' but I doubt the shape is right. What also doesn't jive with that idea is that forty years ago when the child was killed, the officer would already have been in his twenties. That would make your sicko ritual killer a senior citizen."

"By your own logic, then, if the killer's much younger, he couldn't have been more than a kid when this all began forty years ago."

"Touché!" Rikki exclaimed. "You remind me of this rich woman lawyer I met when Austin and I worked a case in the Coachella Valley. I couldn't get her to mind her own business either."

"It's not as if I'm a looky-loo or a nosy journalist trying to get a Pulitzer prize-winning scoop. I have a vested interest in learning everything I can since Dustin Watkins designated me as the next to die." Given the circumstances that had brought us to the hospital, I shut up.

"It appears he got that wrong. To poke a few more holes in your sicko serial killer scenario, although there are some regularities with the murders, there are oddities too. The child's murder and the fire that killed her mother occurred a year apart, not a decade. If the parents were murdered, then the killer resorted to arson, which is a very different choice of weapons than whatever he used to strike his victims on the back of the head. To be a decade apart, the next ritual murder should have occurred in 1989, but there wasn't another one until 1999."

"As far as anyone knows."

"Geez, let's hope that's not true. It would still be a deviation from the pattern if the body was dumped somewhere else. While the murders in 1999, 2009, and 2019 all occurred around the same time of year, the numbers in Billie's notebook that could be months and days are all different. So, there's no set number of days before Labor Day Weekend, a specific cycle of the moon, superstorm, or anything obvious that would add to the ritual idea."

"Touché, back at you," I said, acknowledging Rikki's points. "What's happened to Rachel Lincoln doesn't fit the pattern either."

"One of the reasons I wanted to have this chat with you is to hear what you made of Rachel's dying declaration." I gulped, realizing that may well have been what it was.

"She wanted to get the guilt off her chest—more about what she claims she didn't know than what she did."

"That's the gist of what I got from listening in on your brief conversation. Even with the wire you were wearing, Rachel spoke so softly at times, I couldn't catch it all. We'll transcribe the recording and we'll ask you to go over a written copy to fill in as many of the garbled words as you can. Do you believe she didn't know, until recently, that the driver of the car was kin?" Rikki asked.

"If she was unburdening her conscience, I don't see why she'd lie," I argued. "Technically, though, if the driver of the Camaro was Uncle Link, that makes him Bud Lincoln's kin, not Rachel's. Rachel was a Lincoln by marriage and Penney was a Lincoln because her stepfather adopted her. Rachel never clarified what she meant by kin, so we still can't be certain she was referring to Uncle Link. Rachel did say she was sorry that 'Bud made me do it.' Although she didn't explicitly say what 'it' was, I'm guessing Rachel's husband was behind the confusing information given to the police. Not wanting to implicate a family member could have been a reason for his being less than truthful with the police."

"Judge Brinkley was closed-mouth about it, but he wasn't sure whose idea it had been to hire him. Maybe

Rachel Lincoln was more assertive a couple of decades ago, but my guess is that hiring a lawyer was a decision she would have left up to her husband."

"Her shock at learning that her daughter had been murdered was genuine, Rikki. If Bud Lincoln suspected Uncle Link had killed his stepdaughter, he kept Rachel in the dark about his suspicions."

"If we believe Rachel, Penney kept it secret from her too. The only reason I can imagine that the 'boy crazy' Penney Lincoln kept her relationship with Uncle Link from her mother is that it wasn't an appropriate one. As you've pointed out, Penney wasn't a Lincoln by birth so he wasn't really her uncle, but he must have been much older than she was at almost fifteen."

"Jesse figured the guy in the car was a 'college boy' in his mid-twenties, but if he's the same guy involved in the first murder in 1979, he was older than that. That alone could have gotten Uncle Link into trouble with the law if Penney had decided to tell Mom. Maybe he stopped her," I said. "I wasn't there when Rachel Lincoln ran away from you and Dahlia, but from what she'd said before fainting on the stage, your questions about a black Camaro triggered her meltdown. Is that when she learned the driver was kin?" I asked.

"Not from us. We never said a word about kin because I hadn't read Austin's report from his interview with the Chief yet. I don't know how she reached that conclusion."

"She somehow connected the dots. It was important to her for me to believe she didn't know the driver of the car was kin when Penney left with him."

"I heard her say, 'he's like Bud,' was she referring to the driver?"

"The doctor had stepped back into the room, and she pointed at him and added, 'See his hand?' The doctor must have thought she was talking about him, because he shoved his hands into the pockets of his smock. I asked her again, but she didn't answer me. The doctor's a young resident, so I'd have to see pictures of Bud Lincoln in his late twenties or early thirties to know if there's a resemblance."

"Maybe it was a gesture she was talking about, not his features," Rikki said. "The car might be easier to find than another Lincoln or another Watkins. We have someone running a program to check ownership records. Sad to say, but it's easier to hide the birth—and maybe the death—of a child than to drive without registering a car. We haven't found birth records for a boy named Dustin Watkins or any girl with the last name Watkins."

"Doctor Kennedy said he didn't deliver the child or his sister, but he wasn't the only doctor in the area in the late seventies. The Watkins were recluses so she could have had the children at home on her own, or maybe with the help of a midwife."

"Who knows? There are so many missing puzzle pieces." Rikki rubbed her temples.

"When you were trying to help her yesterday, Rikki, you mentioned the Sitter. Rachel responded as though you meant a babysitter rather than a grave sitter as Dustin seemed to use it. What if 'sitter,' as in babysitter is correct?" I asked. "Dustin and his sister were so young at the time, maybe the parents had a sitter who cared for the kids while they worked in the fields all day."

"That makes as much sense as anything else," Rikki

said. "Even though we don't know her maiden name, Dustin's mother could have had family who sent someone to help once the children were born. A teenaged boy could have helped in the fields and with other tasks, as well as watching the children."

"Diane is still digging through records in Children's Services, but so far, she's found nothing. When his sister died in 1979, they both would have been too young, but before the fire in 1980, Dustin should have been registered for kindergarten."

"I'm not surprised. Are you, Lily? If they didn't register his birth, I'm sure they weren't worried about the school system coming after them. Not unless a neighbor noticed the children and cared enough to wonder why they never went to school. That wasn't likely to happen."

"I get it. The Watkins were an unusual couple, weren't they?" I asked. Then I smacked my head like Billie had done a couple of times. "Wait a second! Why didn't you correct me when I said those DNA results meant you were looking for another Watkins? Dustin's mother wasn't a Watkins except by marriage! What if she's the missing link between the Watkins and the Lincolns? Maybe Lincoln was her maiden name before she married."

"We found the old deed which listed the owner as William Watkins. There was no mention of a wife. Austin ran a bunch of background checks this morning after he spoke to his informant. He did that before he left the prison parking lot, in case he needed to speak with Chief Little Bigmouth again. In his report he says he came up empty on Lincolns anywhere around here."

"It's too bad that Rachel's husband isn't still alive. One way to see if there are family ties between the Lincolns and the Watkins would be to compare his DNA to Mrs. Watkins' DNA." Rikki stood up so fast, her chair fell over.

"He's dead, but who says there's no DNA? Bud Lincoln didn't die that long ago, and Rachel told us he went through lots of tests. Maybe there are still slides or specimens stored somewhere. If she didn't get rid of all his possessions, there could be DNA on a comb, a jacket or a hat he loved to wear. Even if Rachel's too weak to talk to me, her sister might help. If she understands that she might be able to help us determine who killed her niece and tried to kill her sister, I'll bet she'll do it. If all else fails, we'll exhume the body." She bolted out the door and almost knocked Austin over.

"Austin, get in there and kiss that woman. She's a genius!" Then Rikki wagged her finger at me.

"That doesn't mean you're not a pain in the neck. Don't wait for Dahlia. Austin can drive you home."

"Thank you!" I didn't relish another ride in Dahlia's cruiser. Rikki apparently didn't notice the somber expression on Austin's face. I stood up, dragged him into the room, and shut the door.

"You heard your boss. I'd say that was a direct order. Don't make me file a complaint." When he didn't smile, I grew worried. "What is it, Austin?"

"Rachel Lincoln just died."

"Oh, no. That is so awful. Should I tell Rikki?" I reached for the door handle, and Austin grabbed my hand.

"Dahlia's out there. She'll do it." He held on to my hand.

"How did you get here?"

"When a bulletin was issued to be on the lookout for a

black Camaro heading north, I switched on the sirens and hit it, hoping to meet him as I drove south. About twenty minutes later, I spotted the car. I cut across the median and kept after him even when he nearly ran someone off the road while making a quick exit from the highway. A few minutes later, he crossed into oncoming traffic, and purposely sideswiped a minivan. When they spun out in front of me, I had to slam on my brakes to keep from hitting them. By the time I got around them, I'd lost him. I called in my location, hoping someone would spot him again, and then made sure everyone in the van was okay. While I waited for the local police to show up, I called Dahlia and she explained where you were and why."

"The Sitter's absolutely crazy, isn't he?"

"And getting crazier—if that's possible. Dahlia says there's black paint on Rachel Lincoln's bumper from where the Camaro hit her, driving her off the road, and into a ditch. He's never left that kind of evidence between him and a victim before."

"According to Rikki, Rachel Lincoln suffered a blow to the back of her head. He must have pulled her from the car, and then bludgeoned her."

"Yes, that's also what I meant when I said he's getting crazier. Everything he did this afternoon was vicious, but he also risked revealing himself; and I almost had him. He sure drives like he's had police driver training, although, in his hands, it's a weapon."

"You don't need to explain. Dahlia treated me to a sample of police driving on my way here," I said. "Let's go home."

"Thank God, you're okay," Austin said as he finally followed orders.

18

A Sacred Place

"Austin, why kill Rachel Lincoln after all these years?" I asked when we were almost home.

"I wondered about that. He must have figured she was falling apart and was about to tell us something that would identify him or move the investigation forward one way or another."

"Unfortunately, by the time she spoke to me, she didn't say anything that was very helpful. She said the Camaro was driven by 'kin,' but didn't say who that was. If she'd remained in the hospital, and I'd spoken to her before the accident, I believe she could have given us the name of the driver. I hope her confession brought her some peace. If you're right about his motive for killing her, how could the Sitter have known what a vulnerable condition Rachel Lincoln was in unless he's an insider?"

"Jesse said she was already a wreck twenty years ago when Penney disappeared, so plenty of people could have known she was unstable. Today wasn't her first trip to the ER. In her hysterical state, who knows what she told people at the hospital last night when she learned someone had murdered her daughter? One reason Rikki and Dahlia gave up on restricting your movements is that word has already leaked to the public that Penney Lincoln is dead. Ms. Wainwright's fate won't be a secret much longer, either."

"How awful for Roslyn and her family. Does the media know Penney's body was found at The Calla Lily Vineyards?"

"Probably. If you're worried about the paparazzi, they'll end up like Billie if they try to scale an eight-foot fence topped with barbed wire."

"Promise?" I snapped. "They'll have a heyday if they get their hands on me in Slimy Chic. I wonder what it'll take to get my diva pals to destroy those photographs."

"Don't ask me. I don't know any of them well enough to understand what makes them tick." Austin paused as if he was stewing about something I'd said. "Even if you're right and it's an insider, this became a large complex investigation so quickly that we're talking about dozens and dozens of people. There must be two or three dozen police officers from several different jurisdictions involved who stepped in to help given all the people in Lydia Wainwright and Penney Lincoln's lives the police needed to track down and interview. They interviewed some of them more than once. I don't suppose Jesse mentioned that, given his criminal record, he was questioned again."

"Oh, no. He's never going to be able to leave his past behind, is he?" I griped. "He's not old enough to have killed the child or set the fire at the Watkins' place."

"You know Dahlia, she's got her own way of viewing things. Rikki's onboard with the idea of a single killer, but

Dahlia's still considering the possibility of a copycat killer. She hasn't ruled out Dustin Watkins as a suspect, either. When I told Rikki the Chief claims Penney Lincoln called Dustin, Rain Man, she thought that it fit. She's convinced Dustin is autistic."

"Diane also mentioned that possibility and was going to dig around in the records about "Special Needs" children provided services. Pointless now that we know his parents didn't even register his birth."

"I'm sorry I lost the guy in the Camaro. I had about ten seconds in which I could have rammed him, but I didn't want to risk hurting more innocent people."

"You did your best. I wouldn't want you to spend the rest of your life feeling that you'd contributed to the injury or death of an innocent bystander." Then a happy thought occurred to me. "If the dispatcher put out that APB or BOLO or whatever you call it—they had a license plate number for the car, right?"

"Yes, but don't get too excited. The car's registered to the LLC that purchased the Watkins' property. Since the driver of the car is suspected of using the car in the commission of serious crimes, Rikki's asked for a warrant to access the name of the owner."

"Arrgh! It's one step forward and two steps back," I said as we pulled up to the gate. A huge, beefy man I'd never seen before stepped in front of the car even though the arm was up to admit us. He wore a gun in a shoulder holster. The cavalry had arrived. The black t-shirt and pants he wore were a giveaway.

"Good evening, Ms. Callahan, Deputy," he added as he spoke through the window Austin rolled down. "Peter

March sends his regards. I'm Glen Avery. I'm here with two colleagues to keep watch until our boss can meet with you Tuesday morning. If you want us to escort you somewhere, we'll do it. Otherwise, we'll be carrying out surveillance. Not that you'll notice us if we're doing our job right."

"Thank you so much. Has anyone tried to get in here this afternoon?"

"A couple of people who claimed to be reporters, but when I picked up the big guns, they left." He nodded his head in the direction of a rifle with a scope leaning against a post and another "big gun" on the ground. It made me feel queasy. I'm not a fan of guns, big or small. "A moving van left a few minutes ago. He seemed in a hurry to leave—from what he said, he's not a fan of the local police."

"Is there still an officer on the property?" I asked.

"Yes. When my men made the rounds, they spoke to Officer Jim Brady. He said his boss had asked him to escort you to dinner, which is why I didn't insist that we do it. I guess the police weren't sure the deputy would get here in time to join you for dinner."

"Okay, we know Jim Brady and I have no doubt his boss *insisted* that he accompany us. With Jim and the deputy as escorts, we can probably get to dinner and back safely. It'll be wonderful to come home and not be worried another intruder is roaming the property. I'm happy to meet you and glad you're here." I meant every word. After living for years in a mega-city, I never dreamed I'd be worried about a serial killer while living in a small town.

"No problem." When he turned away, I noticed another gun protruding from his waistband. As we drove up the road, I tried to spot his comrades, but to no avail.

"I'm back you guys." I hollered when Austin and I dashed into the house. "Look who I brought with me!" Judy and Billie came running.

"Lily, come meet the secret agents. They already know Austin." He grabbed my hand, and when we entered the kitchen, two large men in black were drinking coffee and eating cookies. Jim was sitting there too, and he smiled when we came into the room.

"Sorry to hear you've had more trouble, ma'am," one of them said as he introduced himself and his partner. The divas were hovering like honeybees in a flower garden.

"It's nice to meet you," I said. We just spoke to Glen at the entry gate. I guess Jim told you he's going to be our escort this evening, along with Marshal Jennings." Jim nodded as I said that.

"Glad to see you, Austin!" They took turns shaking Austin's hand.

"We heard you made a detour on the way home," one of them said. As quickly as they'd said their names, I'd lost track of which man was which given how much alike they were. "I'm sorry your quarry got away."

"I am too. It won't be long now before he's caught. He's become desperate and erratic, and he's making mistakes. Jim and his colleagues are on alert."

"Not just us," Jim added. "The entire county's searching for him. Authorities in adjacent counties, too. The California Highway Patrol has the Camaro on their watch list. We've set up checkpoints and roadblocks in strategic places. He's boxed in unless he already left the area." The two men stood up.

"If you don't need us, we ought to get to work. Thanks for the coffee and cookies," one of the not-so-secret agents said.

"And those gorgeous smiles too," the second man said, winking at my posse members. Zelda fanned herself with her hands.

"If you need me, just whistle. You know how to do that, don't you, Steve? Just put your lips together and blow."

"*To Have or Have Not*—love that movie, sweetheart," Steve said as he took a step toward the backdoor.

"Sweetheart" came out sounding like Humphrey Bogart. Zelda, on the other hand, had not sounded anything like Lauren Bacall. When she's angry or excited, what's left of her Puerto Rican accent becomes more pronounced. "You" comes out more like "Chu." She was obviously enthusiastic about our new helpers.

"I'll go with you, while Lily gets her friends ready to go out for dinner," Austin said as he opened the backdoor and led them out onto the deck.

"Be still my beating heart. Sisters, we've been hanging out in the wrong part of California, haven't we?" Zelda asked. Then she cast a flirty grin toward Jim. "Jim's no slouch in the looks department, either, is he?"

"Stop, or I'll have to place you under arrest for harassing a tired, old cop." Jim laughed. "You heard what Austin said, if you want to go out to eat, you'd better get ready."

"It's not usually too hard to find a place to eat on a Sunday night, but this is a holiday weekend, and there are lots of us," Jim said. "I made reservations for seven at Bistro Benini. They have good food, including pizza and spaghetti, that Billie will love. They can squeeze us in on the terrace, which is my favorite spot. I hope it's okay, Lily."

"Jim, you're wonderful. Thank you. I recently had lunch there with other Calla Lily Winery Board Members and the food was delicious." Pricy as I recall, but what the heck? Jim's single and works hard; why not spend his extra cash on fine dining?

"Where's Mick, Julie?" I asked.

"He was in such a hurry to get here that he didn't sleep at all last night. I told him to take a nap, and I'd call him when it was time for dinner. I've never known Mick to miss a meal, so he'll hustle over here. Jim's right that we'd better get moving if we don't want to be late. In case you hadn't noticed, Lily, you live in the boonies."

"True. Call Mick and tell him the dress is casual, and to meet us here in twenty minutes. Does that work for everyone else?"

"Pizza always works for me," Billie replied.

"Put on your sweatshirt with the hoodie, okay? It'll be chilly once the sun goes down. Tomorrow morning, I'm taking you shopping for school clothes."

"Yes, Number One Mom," Billie said.

"We all have mom numbers," Julie informed me.

"I don't have a number since there's only one granny in the house," Judy added. Her sweet face crinkled with laughter as Billie hugged her. Getting everyone into as few cars as possible was something of a challenge, but we managed. Billie was absolutely over the moon when Jim offered to let him ride in the front of the police cruiser with him.

"No high-speed, police driving, please," I begged Jim.

"Aw, that's no fun," Billie responded.

"We can't keep up, and you're supposed to be our escort, remember?"

"That's true, isn't it? With Zelda driving, if we go too fast, she'll start waving her hands around, and who knows what will happen? We'd better take it easy on them, Jim."

"Whatever you say, partner. Buckle up!" When we got close to the restaurant, Jim turned on his siren and signaled where to turn in. I'm sure Billie loved it.

The restaurant turned out to be a perfect place for our large, rowdy group. It was a lovely evening outdoors, and only once or twice did I peek over my shoulder, worried that someone was sneaking up on me. The menu wowed my Hollywood divas, which is hard to do given that LA is a foodie mecca. So is Napa.

I'm not sure how the subject came up, but when Austin mentioned that Napa was a word used by the Wappo tribe that meant 'plenty.' Billie had another surprise for me. The first surprise was that he'd ordered grilled octopus as an appetizer. Even more surprising was that he ate it.

"Wait until I tell Brandy I ate octopus!" he said. Anyway, his third surprise was most unexpected.

"The Wappo tribe put a curse on the watering hole behind the Watkins' place."

"A curse, how do you know about that?" Zelda asked.

"All of us kids know about it. Everybody says to stay away from the entire area. My parents told me the Wappo poisoned the water, and the folks who lived there went crazy from drinking it. Nobody's lived there for a hundred years, and the curse is even older than that. There's a huge cave underground where the Wappo used to dance and fill it with spirits. Some of them couldn't get out." For some reason, that resonated with Dustin's fears about his sister getting out of her grave. Maybe he'd heard Billie's story, too.

"You're giving me the shivers," Zelda said as she crossed herself. Then she grabbed the cross hanging around her neck. "All we need is evil spirits. The human stinkers around here have been bad enough."

"Ghosts?" Mick asked as his eyes grew wide. He'd been too busy devouring the figs and prosciutto, heirloom tomatoes, and mandilli created with fresh house-made silk handkerchief pasta, to say a word. Don't tell me the guy who'd had no hesitation about joining us in the middle of a murder investigation was afraid of ghosts. Then he shrugged and went back to eating.

"I've lived around here longer than you have, Billie, and I know for a fact there were people on that property more recently than a hundred years ago," Judy said. "I don't believe in curses, but bad water can make people sick, so that's interesting."

"What did you hear about the curse when you were growing up, Judy?" Julie asked. I wasn't surprised the story piqued the interest of my writer friend.

"Some hogwash about the family that settled there being cursed because the land was sacred. Almost anything in nature could have been sacred to the Wappo or most other native people. Like a natural spring if that's what fed the watering hole that Billie's talking about. Unusual stone formations and caves too, especially if they offered shelter, or places with abundant food sources. That's why Napa works as a name for the valley which means the entire valley is a sacred place."

"Well, I recently learned some of the tribes practiced kuksu," Austin added. Their ceremonies included dance; some of which took place underground, so that part of Billie's story could be true."

"If the entire valley is regarded as a place of plenty, we're all on sacred ground. Does that mean we're all cursed?" Jim asked.

"That's my point, Jim. The curse idea is ridiculous. Based on what happened to the Wappo tribe, I'm afraid they're the ones who were cursed. Now if you told me that squabbling about who got to use the watering hole led to some idiot poisoning it rather than sharing it, and it killed them all, I could believe that. The Watkins' property never was very productive, although Billie's right that no one has tried to do anything with it for decades. Maybe there's poison in the watering hole that seeped into the soil and ruined the crops or drove the people mad. That has nothing to do with the spirits or curses, Billie."

"I'm glad you've stayed away from there, son," Jim said. "Judy's right that nothing good has come from the place as long as I've been alive."

"Oh, no, do you think Dustin's been there, and that's why he doesn't seem right?"

"I don't know, Billie. Some people are born with problems like Dustin's. Diane's trying to find out if anyone's ever heard of a boy named Dustin who was diagnosed with autism before everyone lost track of him."

"I hope someone figures out where he's gone before the Sitter hurts him anymore."

"I hope so, too, Billie." I put an arm around him, and he leaned against me and whispered.

"I'm pretty sure I know where Dustin is. Can Austin and the secret agents go look for him?"

"Hmm. We'll ask Austin about it when we get home. For now, let's keep this between us, okay?" Then, true to his twelve-year-old priorities, he piped up.

"What's for dessert?"

19

The Shack

WHEN WE LEFT for home after dinner, Zelda insisted that it was her turn to ride in the police cruiser—in the front seat since she'd never done that before. Billie was a little disappointed, but I was grateful it worked out that way. Mick took the extra seat in the car the divas had driven, so Billie rode with Judy, Austin, and me.

"Billie has a question for you, Austin," I said as soon as we left the restaurant parking lot. "He thinks he knows where Dustin might be."

"Not in that poisonous watering hole, I hope," Judy said.

"No, not there. I told you I never went to the watering hole. I did sort of get lost in the area once when I was exploring the woods."

"Were you following Dustin?" I asked.

"This was before I knew about Dustin. Two years ago, at least. When I realized where I was, I got really scared. Sort of like what you said, Judy. There was a creek and I wondered if it was connected to the watering hole. Then I thought what if the poison was in the air too."

"So, what makes you believe Dustin might be around there?" Austin asked.

"I climbed to the top of a big pile of boulders to see where I was. That's how I know for sure that I was in the woods behind the Watkins' property. When I searched around me, I saw this broken-down old shack. I thought people might have lived there until the poison killed them. The wind blew and a big cloth filled up with air. One end was tied to the shack and others to posts in the ground with rope. Now I wonder if some of the garbage lying around was too new to be a hundred years old. What if that was a tent and Dustin's living in it?"

"That's a good question. Was the shack very far from the road?" Austin asked.

"Yes. A car went by, and it was tiny, but there was a trail. I smelled horses, so I thought it was for horseback riding. It might be big enough for your SUV or Judy's truck. I'm not sure."

"When you were on top of the boulders in back of the Watkins' property, was the road to your right or your left?" Austin asked.

"To my right. There were huge oaks everywhere, so I don't know how easy it would be to see the trail or anything else from the road. The Watkins' place wasn't straight in front of me either. It was more on my left."

"I've been looking at maps of the preserve area around the Calla Lily Vineyard. Let me see if I can locate the place you're describing and get a better idea of the best way to get in there."

"Then will you and the agents go look for Dustin? The Sitter would never win a fight against you." Billie was almost pleading with Austin at this point.

"I can't promise until I've done my research and spoken to Rikki about it. I don't see what harm it could do to check it out."

"You'll have to be sneaky, so Dustin and the Sitter don't see you coming until the last minute. I don't want Dustin to get scared and run away or the Sitter to see you coming and hurt Dustin. It might be easier to do that at night."

"Not tonight, kiddo," I said. "You heard what Austin said about needing to do his homework. Sneakiness requires careful planning."

"Maybe tomorrow night since we're shopping for clothes in the morning, Number One Mom!"

"I'll wake you up early so we can beat the crowds. Labor Day is a huge sale day."

"Not without me," Austin said. By the time we drove the last few miles for home, Billie was almost asleep. When we drove in through the gates, he woke up and searched for the secret agents.

"They're good," he said.

I hoped Billie was right if they decided to undertake the mission he'd proposed to Austin. Rikki had called Austin soon after we returned home from dinner. She thought checking out the shack was worth doing if they could locate it.

The reason she'd called Austin was to update him about the effort to identify the victim who might be a Lincoln. Rachel Lincoln's sister had wasted no time providing Rikki with items that had belonged to Bud Lincoln. The crime lab had prepared samples in a couple of hours. By morning they might know if Mrs. Watkins was, in fact, a member of the Lincoln family.

I slept better that night than I had since this entire nightmare began. I woke up happy at the prospect of playing mom by taking Billie shopping. When I got to the kitchen, Judy was already there, of course, and coffee was made. When she saw me, a quizzical look came over her face.

"Lily, what are you doing here? Did you forget something?"

"What do you mean?"

"Billie said Jim was taking the two of you shopping. Since you were already in the front seat, Billie was excited that he was going to get to ride in the back this time."

"Austin!" I shouted. I ran up the stairs, but Aunt Lettie's room was empty. No Austin. No Billie.

"Where is he?" I asked as divas stumbled from their rooms.

"Who?"

"Austin!" I replied.

"Judy, did Austin go with Billie?" I yelled that question, but Judy had followed me upstairs and stood right behind me.

"I don't think so. Maybe he's already gone after him, though," she said. "I'll call Jesse." We both ran downstairs to the landline in the kitchen. Judy had Jesse on the phone in a second.

"Jesse says Austin, Steve, and Glen left ten minutes ago."

"Was that before or after Billie left?" I asked.

"About the same time," Judy replied. "What, Jesse?"

"Jesse says they had maps with them, and you're not supposed to go anywhere."

"Let me speak to Jesse, please," I insisted.

"Jesse, did you see Jim Brady leave?"

"Yes. Austin saw him, too. Billie was in the back, and that's when Austin and the others took off after Jim."

"Did Billie seem scared?" I asked.

"Not really. He was smiling and trying to get attention, I think, by waving. I'm sorry I let Jim in here. He said Dahlia sent him to pick up important materials she'd left in the reading room."

"Jim lied to Billie and Judy too. That's why Billie got into the backseat of his car."

"What can I do?" Jesse asked.

"What did they tell you to do?" I asked.

"Block the gate with my truck and don't allow anyone in or out—that includes you."

"Call me if you get any news." When I hung up the phone, Melody stood there already dressed.

"Did you find Billie?" She asked.

"No, but Austin and a couple of the men went after him."

"Lily! Lily!" Carrie and Julie came running into the kitchen. Zelda was following them.

"You've got to see this," Julie said. "When Billie told us that he thought no one was living at the Watkins' place for a hundred years, I thought maybe that's when the trouble started—a hundred years ago. Carrie said we needed to dig into old news about Calistoga. We worked until about four this morning. She has access to all sorts of archives. Look."

The man in the photo was the spitting image of Jim Brady if you ignored the ratty looking hair that hung to his shoulders. As far as I could tell, this photo was taken right before he was hung. The caption read:

Bart Lincoln sentenced to hang for claim jumping and the murder of Hank Watkins.

"Look behind the condemned man," Carrie demanded. Another man stood in front of an opening in an outcropping of large boulders. Water poured from a crevice in the rocks. The man had a slick grin on his face as he stood there glaring.

"What do you want to bet that's another member of the Watkins clan?" Julie asked.

"This can't be about gold a hundred years later. If there had been gold, the Watkins would have cleaned it out," I argued.

"Yeah, and they wouldn't have lived like paupers on that miserable plot of land they owned before someone torched what little they had and killed them. Revenge is more durable than gold," Judy added.

"Some members of the clans may have tried to end the conflict." I explained about the DNA evidence and the possibility that Mrs. Watkins was a Lincoln and that the still unidentified victim was also a Lincoln.

"From that photo, it's clear Jim Brady's a Lincoln," I said, feeling sick at the thought that he had Billie.

"By marrying a Watkins, maybe you weren't a Lincoln anymore and Jim Brady set that fire to settle the score. How could Jim Brady be a serial killer? I've known him most of his life." Judy looked every bit her age as she leaned against the kitchen island.

Marlowe suddenly went nuts, growling and barking at the door that leads into the kitchen from the cellar. I grabbed a huge French knife from a drawer in the island. When the doorknob turned slowly, someone spoke, and I recognized his voice as he opened the door.

"Lily, you have to come with me. Fast, the short way! We need to save the boy. The lawman that boy shot too, or his number's up." Dustin took my hand. "The Sitter set a trap, but I know how to fix it—by the numbers. You have to get the boy while I do the numbers."

"Dustin, it's okay. I can call Austin to tell him it's a trap, okay?" I dialed Austin's phone and it rang—upstairs.

"Judy, call Jesse. Have him call Glen and tell them they're walking into a trap." I stepped toward the cellar door.

"Lily, no. Austin told you to stay here," Judy said. She was already calling Jesse.

"Who knows where they are by now?" I grabbed a kitchen towel and wrapped it around the knife. Marlowe ran down the stairs.

"Oh, no, you don't! If you go, I go," Zelda said as she grabbed a paring knife and a rolling pin from a counter. She swung the rolling pin like it was a baseball bat. Carrie and Julie grabbed knives, too, and wrapped them as I'd done.

"Are you telling me you lived in LA as long as you did, and none of you carry mace?" Melody asked as she pulled a can from a crossbody shoulder bag she wore with Darjeeling's little head poking out. I heard Judy leave a message for Jesse.

"Hurry," Dustin said. "I can show you where the Sitter hides his guns."

"Aren't you going to call Jesse again?" I asked Judy.

"And let you all take off without me? Not one of you knows how to handle a gun like I do!"

Dustin led us down into the cellar and left using a door I never even knew was there.

"Don't look at me," Judy said. "I didn't know it was here."

"Our security has more holes than Swiss Cheese," I muttered. Dustin ran catty-cornered to the fence not far from the slime pit. He knocked a piece of the fence right over.

As soon as we were in the woods, Dustin picked up the pace and we moved as fast as we could without stumbling over fallen limbs or other obstacles in our path. At least it was daylight and we could see where we were going.

I'd never ventured into this section of the woods, so I only had a vague idea of where we were and where we were headed. When Dustin said the "short way," I could only imagine he had us crossing along the diagonal of a square or rectangle while Jim, and the men following him, were forced to take the long way around the perimeter using roads. We didn't have to cut across the entire diagonal, either, to reach the area where Jim had set his trap.

We couldn't have been moving for more than twenty minutes, but my legs felt like rubber. My friends were breathing as hard as I was. Only Judy seemed to be moving with ease. Marlowe was in the zone. I figured at the pace we'd set, closer to a jog than a walk, we'd already covered a couple of miles.

After another ten minutes, I didn't think I could go on. When we reached an outcropping of granite, I prayed we'd arrived at our destination. Dustin turned and pointed toward a narrow ridge trail that ran along behind the granite protrusion.

"Quiet now so I can hear. Marlowe, shh!" Then he started up the ridge that could only accommodate us single file. As we trudged on and on, climbing higher and higher, I wanted to look around to see if I could spot the Watkins' place or the shack. The rock obstructed the view to my right, and the drop off to my left stopped me from looking in that direction.

We finally started to head down the other side and were soon wedged between rock on both sides. I felt relieved until Dustin suddenly disappeared. Judy and Marlowe vanished next. When I reached the same point, I could see that the trail split. I could have continued around large rocks in my path where the trail began to rise again. Instead, I took a branch that descended sharply into a cleft in the rock.

"That's the trap," Dustin said as we followed him to another opening in the rock wall. He pointed to a crudely fashioned bomb made from sticks of dynamite triggered by a timer. It sat on a large flat rock slap. If the bomb went off, anyone passing beneath it would be buried in stone. "I can fix the numbers. You get Billie. I'll show you where to hide. The guns are there." Judy walked to a narrow opening in the stone and removed a rifle and a pistol. Zelda tossed the rolling pin away.

"No noise!" Dustin whispered.

"That's a .38 isn't it?" Zelda asked Judy in a whisper. Judy nodded. "I got this." In a few more minutes, we were all in place as Dustin scrambled out onto the ledge, and went to work on the timer. He scooted back into hiding and none too soon.

"For a serial killer, you're awfully dumb, Jim," Billie said, loudly. I could hear him, but I couldn't see him.

"Shut up! I've had just about all I can stand of your mouth."

"So? Do you think Ms. Wainwright wanted to hear you run your mouth?"

"I said, shut up! Or I'll…"

"What? You'll kill me like you killed my teacher? I'm the bait, remember? They're not going to come after you unless they hear my big mouth screaming 'help.'" I cringed as I heard Jim slap Billie. I moved to go get him. Dustin grabbed my arm and shook his head.

"What a wimp!" Billie hollered. "My dad slaps me way harder than that!"

"Up there," Jim said, "Or I'll take my chances yelling help without you." I heard the gritty scraping of footsteps on rock. They must be coming up an incline or climbing over rocks from the other side. Billie was silent for an agonizing minute or two.

"Ow! I'm going. This is the dumbest thing you've ever done. You know why? Because I bet Austin and his crack team are already up there. Yee-haw, Austin, it's Billie-the-kid. I've got the idiot with me who's convinced he can outwit you." Just then some member of our group shifted, and a slew of gravel trickled down the rock.

"What'd I tell you? Watch out, below Jim!" I heard

what sounded like a spray of rocks and gravel. Boots skidded on the rocks.

"You delinquent! I'll teach you…"

"Let go!" Billie shouted. He must have kicked Jim who grunted. His grunting was followed by more skidding. This time I also heard someone skittering on up the rocks and getting closer to us. When I saw Billie's face, I couldn't wait another second. I slipped out, yanked him toward me, and then dragged him backward with me into the space where we were hiding. Less than a minute later, Jim appeared.

"Come out, come out, wherever you are. You're going to miss the showdown. Don't you want to see Austin get what he has coming to him? Lily's going to pay and pay and pay for screwing up my plans. If she'd stayed indoors where she belonged, I would have had the evidence cleaned up by morning."

"You're delusional, Jim. You know what I hate more than a serial killer? A dirty cop serial killer." That was Austin speaking in his old west marshal voice. Jim pointed his gun upward, and Dustin lunged at him. The rifle clattered as it fell to the ground.

"You're not my Sitter anymore!" Dustin cried. Jim fell backward and grabbed Dustin by the hoodie he had on. They'd landed on the flat rock and rolled toward the edge. Zelda and I were out on our bellies in a flash. We each grabbed an ankle and held onto Dustin as Billie and the Divas grabbed us. Marlowe squeezed between us, ran up over Dustin's back, and snarled and snapped at Jim. Startled, Jim let go and dropped thirty or forty feet. I don't believe he landed well. We held on as Dustin scooted back toward us, and our friends guided us all back into the hidey hole.

"Hello, lawman," Dustin said when he turned around.

"Well, I'll be ding-danged if it ain't Ma Tucker and her whole gang," he said shaking his head in disbelief.

"Posse, Marshal," I said as I threw my arms around his neck and gave him a kiss.

20

Untangling the Vines

JIM BRADY SURVIVED the fall, but he wasn't going to be able to hurt anyone ever again. It would be weeks before the police could question him. In the meantime, with help from a few additional sources, Austin, Rikki, and Dahlia were doing their best to piece together the story behind Jim Brady's lifetime of vicious outbursts.

Among Bud Lincoln's boxed items Rachel had stashed in the garage was an old address book with information about several Lincoln family members. They were only able to locate one of them. Rikki and Diane had driven to a small town several hours away to speak to an elder member of the Lincoln family who'd outlived many of the younger Lincolns.

"The first thing Great Aunt Mildred told us was that the Lincolns and the Watkins had buried the hatchet soon after Bart Lincoln was hanged. She scoffed at the idea that there was ill will between the two families. Bart Lincoln was a bad man and both sides of the family were glad to see him go."

"Well that does away with family vengeance as a motive for James Brady's viciousness," Carrie said.

"Yes, it does. According to his great aunt, James Brady Lincoln was twelve years old when his parents sent him to help at the Watkins' place. Dustin and his sister, Molly, were twins, and the home birth had been hard on their mother, who never fully recovered. As the children grew older, it became more difficult to care for them. Not only did Dustin have problems, but his twin sister did as well. Dustin says he tried to help Molly by counting things for her. Sometimes that worked."

"From the way Jim's great aunt described their behavior, these days they would have been diagnosed with an autism spectrum disorder. Dustin's sister was more impaired than he was, and would often injure herself. It's not uncommon for young children with autism to engage in self-harm, but with intervention, most can grow out of it," Diane explained.

"Why didn't the parents get help from professionals?"

"Apparently, Judy, they were raised in a religious tradition that prohibited seeking medical care from doctors—not Christian Science, but a smaller sect. Their reclusiveness was a way to avoid trouble with the law about their religious beliefs."

"What does this have to do with Jim Brady becoming a serial killer?" Zelda asked.

"While Dustin's not always the best source of information, he explained that the Sitter, as he called him, tried harder and harder to keep them out of trouble. His parents either didn't care or were oblivious, but Jim began to tie them to the bedposts or in chairs. He put pillows on the bedpost to keep the girl from banging her head and made 'fat arms' so she couldn't bite them. Dustin said that meant he wrapped her arms in wet rags that tasted bad. If she pulled them off, Jim tied her arms to her side. He often struck or kicked them."

"That's beyond belief," I said.

"It's difficult for me to hear, too, despite the things I've seen during my career at Children's Services. Twins are challenging, but with developmental delays or other disabilities, parenting can be overwhelming."

"It couldn't have been any easier for a twelve-year-old!" I declared. Billie was a self-reliant child for his age, but I couldn't conceive of the idea that he could be left alone to care for three or four-year-old twins for hours. "Jim Brady must have been desperate and angry to do what he did to the children. I can't see how it made Dustin's sister easier to handle."

"Dustin said Molly didn't like it. She scratched, bit, and kicked him. One day after she bit him, he hit her with an iron doorstop. Dustin still says it was his fault, which is what he told his parents. The family buried her in the woods, far away from their place. A year later, on the anniversary of her death, Jim told Dustin she was coming back to kill them all out of revenge. Shortly after that warning, the fire broke out. Dustin, who was searching for his sister, wasn't inside when the house went up in flames, but the blast was so strong, it threw him away from the house."

"How awful! I wonder why Jim didn't leave rather than turning into a killer."

"He tried. Soon after he arrived, he ran off and called his mom, asking her to let him come home. He was severely rebuked, and when he returned to the Watkins' place, 'he probably got what was coming to him' according to his great aunt. He never called them again. In fact, he never returned home at all," Rikki explained.

"That was harsh," Zelda said. "He was trapped, wasn't he?"

"He could have gotten help from us," Diane responded, "but for a child who was brought up to see the authorities as untrustworthy, he really was trapped."

"After the house burned down and they took Dustin to the hospital in San Francisco, Jim followed him there. Jim was only fourteen, so he didn't last long as an underage kid on the streets. When he was picked up as a runaway, he must have dropped Lincoln and became James Brady," Rikki said. "Austin found a driver's license issued to him using that name a few years later."

"We found a birth certificate for James Brady," Austin commented. "As clever as he was, Jim could easily have found someone to make him a fake one."

"True. More than one, perhaps." Rikki added. "Not long after he was issued the driver's license, Jim visited a group home where Dustin Watkins had eventually been placed. They believed he was James Watkins, Dustin's brother. For years, Jim visited Dustin as James Watkins, while he earned a GED, an associate degree in criminology, and became a police officer as James Brady."

"Don't tell me he visited Dustin because he felt guilty or responsible for the fact that he was so badly burned in the fire," Zelda asserted. "I won't believe it."

"No. Dustin said Jim visited him for help with numbers. When Diane asked what kind of help, Dustin said 'numbers to win guessing games.'"

"He meant gambling, didn't he?" Zelda asked.

"Yes, he did," Rikki replied.

"That's a believable reason for a man like Jim to take an interest in the Numbers Man," Melody added as she passed the pizza around again. Billie would have loved it, but he was having dinner with Brandy and her family. We'd taken his absence as an opportunity to untangle the twisted vines of the Watkins-Lincoln family ties and bring closure to a mystery forty years in the making.

"I'm not sure that was his original reason for visiting Dustin. He may have just been interested in finding out what Dustin remembered or believed about the circumstances surrounding his family's deaths. Anyway, Jim brought cards and taught Dustin how to play hearts, and when Dustin 'learned fast,' he moved on to blackjack and poker. He got permission to take Dustin on outings, picked up Dustin, and took him to tribal casinos where, from what we've learned, Jim often won big." That was Dahlia chiming in. She'd been relatively quiet and on her best behavior tonight—so far.

"Dustin didn't mind being seen in the casino?" I asked.

"No," Diane said as she jumped into the conversation. "In fact, he was often treated special because he was different—his behavior as well as his appearance."

"Eventually, when Dustin turned eighteen, Jim moved him out of the group home and brought him back to the Calistoga area. By then, Jim had used some of his winnings to purchase the Watkins' property, hiding his ownership behind the LLC. He'd fixed up the shack for Dustin, and parked his pricy Camaro there most of the time, covering it with a tarp."

"When did he move the body of Mrs. Watkins into the grave with her daughter?" Carrie asked.

"What I want to know is why?" Judy added.

"He was still manipulating Dustin by using the old threats that his sister would get out and kill again if Dustin didn't keep watch. Dustin suggested she might rest better if her mother was with her. At some point, Jim dug up Mrs. Watkins' body from where her sister had buried her in a small family plot on the property, and moved her to Molly's gravesite."

"That's gross," Melody said. "I can't believe Jim would have done that to make Dustin feel better. What was really going on?"

"Penney Lincoln's what was going on," Dahlia replied. "Jim was on patrol in his cruiser and picked her up one night for being out after curfew. When he dropped her at home, we think Bud must have recognized him, and maybe Penney overheard her stepdad talking to someone about it."

"How?" I asked wondering if that's what had happened to Rachel Lincoln the day that she'd fainted onstage. Jim had been sitting in a front-row seat near the stage.

"He has a birthmark on his left hand that's distinctive. We asked his great aunt about it, and she said it's common among the Lincoln men. That could have caught Bud's attention," Diane replied.

"If Penney's stepdad also had the same mark on his hand, maybe that's all it took for her to put two and two together. Unless Jim tells us, we may never know for sure.

Dustin said she called Jim 'Uncle Link,' which made Jim angry."

"That could be the incident my informant in prison witnessed right before Penney Lincoln went missing. Jim was in the Camaro, though, not his police cruiser," Austin added. "It's possible Rachel Lincoln wasn't lying when she said she thought someone else was driving the Camaro."

"Why did she lie to her mother?" Jesse asked.

"Dustin said she told the Sitter she needed money," Dahlia replied.

"If she was blackmailing Uncle Link, telling her mother would have let the cat out of the bag," I suggested.

"Yep. She knew him as Officer Jim Brady, so that's how she must have contacted him. He tried to keep his identity hidden by switching to the Camaro when he picked Penney up at school and again later at her home," Dahlia asserted.

"It's no wonder he was angry when my informant saw him chewing Penney out," Austin added. "That couldn't have been too long before she was killed."

"You must be right," Rikki said. "Except for the deaths of the Watkins couple in the fire, the crime lab hasn't pinned down the exact dates the others were killed. Even in Ms. Wainwright's case, she was missing for days before her body was dumped in the drainpipe. So, it's hard to pinpoint when Penney Lincoln was killed in relation to the informant's testimony. I wouldn't be surprised if Jim started up the scary talk about bodies rising from the grave because he had a body, or planned to have a new body, to dump."

"So that's the 1999 murder," I said, sighing deeply.

"I'm guessing Ms. Wainwright became a problem for Jim when she discovered she was pregnant."

"That plus Lydia Wainwright had also seen Jim behind the wheel of the Camaro. According to Dustin, 'she liked numbers, too,' and they'd met at one of the casinos. The two of them were seen several times when they spent the weekend together at a casino farther south. Without Dustin, Jim didn't do so well."

"Amazingly, they were able to keep their affair secret," Julie commented. "She wouldn't have been able to do that much longer since she was pregnant."

"Making their relationship public would have been risky for Jim, too. Lydia had discovered his 'double life' as a gambler with expensive tastes," I said. "He was trapped again."

"Yes, and he got in deeper and deeper each time he came up against a situation in which he found himself trapped," Rikki observed.

"So, what about the unidentified victim with Lincoln family DNA?" I asked.

"Jim's elderly aunt says she's a great-niece who disappeared after visiting the area. Bud Lincoln was still alive then, and the aunt said she'd gone to Calistoga to see Bud and Rachel. When her great aunt called to ask about her whereabouts, Bud and Rachel told her that she must have decided to visit San Francisco instead of going home because they got a postcard from her," Diane said.

"A postcard sent from San Francisco would have been easy enough for Jim to fake," I groused.

"Yes, and Jim's aunt said that's what they thought she'd done at first. Eventually, even though it went against their beliefs, the aunt insisted that they file a missing person report with the San Francisco County Sheriff's Department," Rikki said.

"As you can imagine, that went nowhere," Austin added.

"We're still not clear how it happened—maybe Bud mentioned they had another relative in the area and she looked Jim up. Dustin says a new girl showed up with Jim at the old Watkins' place. Dustin was confused about it because her name was Lincoln, and she called his mother Lincoln and Jim Lincoln instead of Jim Brady. 'Too many Lincolns until Jim told him it was his sister in disguise, trying to confuse them. Anyway, that was the last anyone reported having seen the young woman."

"Poor Dustin. What's going to happen to him?" Melody asked.

"He's been given a thorough physical exam and is being evaluated by a psychiatrist. I doubt he'll be regarded as fit to serve as a witness against Jim Brady, but we have plenty of evidence to convict Jim without Dustin's testimony. We found the murder weapon hidden in the shack."

"Was he trying to pin the murders on Dustin?" Carrie asked Dahlia.

"He may have convinced himself he could do that, but who knows? There's other evidence, including DNA, to tie Jim to the victims. Maybe if this had all ended differently, he could have tampered with the evidence to set Dustin up. You made that impossible once you found the bodies, Lily."

"Jim made it clear he didn't approve when I caught

him glaring at me from the dark. What's amazing is that he could be so calm and civil—smiling and joking even—sitting in our kitchen or dining room while wanting to kill me."

"Dustin warned you he had a bright and shiny face," Judy reminded me. "He was good at playing the mild-mannered, good-natured local police officer."

"I know. Thank goodness Dustin decided not to let Jim hurt Billie or me, and trusted us enough to show us how to help. Although, Austin and his guys probably could have rescued Billie without us."

"Probably?" Austin asked. "Who arrived moments after you did, avoided Jim's trap, and disarmed the bomb?"

"You and your posse," I responded. "Dustin thought he'd stopped the countdown rather than resetting it. Will the prosecutors' office file any charges against Dustin?"

"If he's judged unfit to testify, I doubt they'll find him fit to be bound over as a defendant even if they could figure out what offenses to charge him with," Dahlia responded, stretching her arms above her head.

"He's paid dearly as Jim nearly killed him, abused, manipulated, and kept him confined in the woods for most of his life," Judy said.

"Dustin is going to be placed into the disability service system where he'll get case manager coordinate his care," Diane added. "I'm not sure he'll ever be allowed to live on his own, but you'll be able to visit him."

"As long as he gets to spend some time in the woods, he'll be okay," I murmured, wondering what we could do to make that happen.

"A toast!" I said, jumping up from my seat and picking up my glass of wine. "To closing the case before the case closed the curtain on the Calla Lily Players—before it ever went up. The show must go on!"

Billie burst into the room and looked around as if wondering what he'd missed. Then he spotted pizza! The child is a bottomless pit. Then, again, he's also a perpetual motion machine until he conks out to sleep.

I ran to greet Ron Lewis, Brandy's dad, who I heard laughing in the hallway in his hearty, distinctive way. I glanced around the room, and marveled that, despite the horrible events we'd been assembled to discuss, the air was filled with goodness. I remembered what Judy had said about Aunt Lettie sending Austin to me amid one of the worst moments of my life.

Now, Billie stood there, alive with youthful energy. A testament to resilience, and to the light that can come from even the darkest circumstances. Leonard Cohen has written a beautiful song, *Anthem*, telling us there's a crack in everything and that's how the light gets in.

It's not that song I heard, though. It was Aunt Lettie's soft voice quoting Hemingway as she often did when I was down about something bad that had happened:

"Calla Lily, *'the world breaks everyone and afterward many are strong at the broken places.'* Be strong."

—THE END—

Thank you so much for reading *A Tangle in the Vines* Calla Lily Mystery #2. Please take a moment and leave a review on Amazon, Bookbub, and Goodreads. Reviews are so important when it comes to helping readers know if a book is for them and reviews are vital to me as a writer. Thank you in advance for your support.

There's more to come for Lily, Austin, Marlowe, and their friends. In *Fall's Killer Vintage*, the Taste of Napa Challenge turns out to be more challenging than anyone imagined. One of the wines entered in the competition is more than a little disappointing when it turns out to be a killer vintage. When one of Aunt Lettie's old friends becomes a suspect, Lily is soon caught up in the mystery. Is the murder of a federal judge about a rivalry among vintners, or is someone out for revenge?

Recipes

Crispy Butterscotch Praline Cookies

About 24 cookies

Ingredients

1/2 cup butter, softened
1 cup packed brown sugar
1 large egg
1 teaspoon vanilla extract
1 cup all-purpose flour
1/4 teaspoon salt
1/2 cup pecans, coarsely chopped
1/2 cup butterscotch chips
24 pecan halves

Preparation

Preheat oven to 350° F.

Mix all ingredients except for the pecans and butterscotch chips and blend well.

Fold in the chopped pecans and butterscotch chips, reserving pecan halves.

Drop cookie dough a tablespoon at a time onto ungreased cookie sheets about two inches apart. Press a little and place a half pecan in the center of each cookie.

Bake for 13-14 minutes.

Remove from oven and let the cookies cool.

Mississippi Mud Cookies

36 cookies

Ingredients

<u>Chocolate Cookie</u>
2 sticks butter softened
1 cup light brown sugar
1 cup granulated sugar
2 teaspoons vanilla extract
2 large eggs beaten
2 1/4 cups all-purpose flour
1/2 cup unsweetened cocoa powder
1 teaspoon baking soda
Pinch salt
3 cups miniature marshmallows
3 cups pecans coarsely chopped

<u>Chocolate Frosting</u>
1/2 cup butter
1/3 cup milk
6 tablespoons unsweetened cocoa
3 1/2 cups powdered sugar
1 teaspoon vanilla extract

Preparation

<u>Chocolate Cookie</u>
Preheat the oven to 375° F. Line baking sheets with parchment paper.

Blend the butter, brown sugar, granulated sugar, vanilla and eggs. In a separate bowl, mix the flour, cocoa, baking soda and salt. Gradually add the dry mixture into the wet mixture and blend until combined. Fold in half of the chopped pecans—1 ½ cups.

Drop the dough a tablespoon at a time onto baking sheets, 12 cookies per sheet, and bake 9-10 minutes. Take the baking sheet from the oven and add about 6 miniature marshmallows to each cookie. The cookies are hot so the marshmallows will start to melt and should stick to them.

Return the cookies to the oven for another minute or so. Remove them and top the marshmallows with a teaspoon or so of chopped pecans, pressing lightly so they stay put! Allow the cookies to cool on a baking rack before frosting.

<u>Chocolate Frosting</u>
In a medium saucepan combine butter, milk, and cocoa and place over medium heat. Stir constantly until butter the butter melts and the ingredients are blended. Remove from heat and whisk in the vanilla. Then add half of the powdered sugar and stir until smooth. Add another cup of powdered sugar and stir again before adding the last half cup using a little less or a little more as needed for the frosting to be the consistency that you can drizzle it over the cookies. Using about a tablespoon for each cookie, frost each cookie. If there's frosting left, go back over the cookies again and add more! Allow frosting to cool and set up before serving the cookies.

Molasses Spice Cookies
30 Cookies

Ingredients

3/4 cup butter, melted
1 cup white sugar
1 egg
1/4 cup molasses
1 teaspoon vanilla
2 cups all-purpose flour
2 teaspoons baking soda
1/2 teaspoon salt
1 teaspoon ground cinnamon
1/2 teaspoon ground cloves
1/2 teaspoon ground ginger
1/2 cup demerara sugar

Preparation

In a medium bowl, mix together the melted butter. white sugar, and egg until smooth. Stir in the vanilla and molasses.

Combine the flour, baking soda, salt, cinnamon, cloves, and ginger until well-blended.

Add to the molasses mixture.

Cover, and chill the dough for at least an hour.

Preheat oven to 375° F

Create walnut-sized balls of dough and roll them in the

demerara sugar. Place cookies 2 inches apart onto ungreased baking sheets.

Bake for 8 to 10 minutes in the preheated oven—you want the tops to crack. Cool before serving.

Figs and Prosciutto

Serves 6-8

Ingredients

12 firm ripe figs, stemmed
4 to 6 Ounces fresh goat cheese
12 paper-thin slices prosciutto sliced in half
1 cup arugula
Saba for drizzling [or substitute balsamic vinegar]
Extra-virgin olive oil for drizzling
Freshly ground pepper

Preparation

Preheat oven to 350° F

Slice each fig in half.

Place about a teaspoon of goat cheese in the center of each fig half.

Wrap each stuffed fig half in prosciutto.

Place on a baking sheet and bake 10 minutes.

Remove, allow to cool slightly, and place the baked figs on a platter covered with arugula.

Drizzle with Saba [or a Balsamic Vinegar] & EVO. Sprinkle with fresh ground pepper, to taste, and serve.

About the Author

Dr. Anna Celeste Burke is an award-winning, USA Today & Wall Street Journal bestselling author who enjoys snooping into life's mysteries with fun, fiction, & food—California style! She writes five mystery series set in California: The Jessica Huntington Desert Cities Mystery Series, The Georgie Shaw Cozy Mystery Series, the Corsario Cove Cozy Mystery Series, the Seaview Cottages Cozy Mystery Series, and the Calla Lily Mystery Series. To get the latest news, subscribe to her newsletter at: desertcitiesmystery.com.

Made in the USA
Columbia, SC
10 August 2022